Identity

Deborah Sevilla

Dedicated to Arnel, Samantha, and Jessica

for not just putting up with my insanity

but encouraging it.

Chapter I

Today I will be invisible. Oh yes, it is possible, but not as easy as it seems. I put a little brown temporary dye in my hair to hide my caramel-colored highlights and admired the effortless-looking wisps I created around my face. Dark brown contacts masked my unforgettable, dense blue eyes. A solid, neutral-colored T-shirt, jeans, and black ballet flats made a perfectly normal-looking outfit—nothing that would really stay with someone. Invisible.

Concealed behind what could only be described as an eclectic collection of clothing in my walk-in closet was a long, skinny, hidden drawer. It was probably designed to hold and safeguard valuable jewelry. I stared at the contents. So many to choose from. *Who should I be today?* I wondered, shuffling through an assortment of driver's licenses, passports, and credit cards.

Ah, yes—Ann Jones. Unassuming, easy to say, and easy to spell. A name anyone would forget seconds after she left. I grabbed Ann Jones's ID and credit cards from the drawer and placed them in their designated spots in a plain black phone case. With a boring-looking book in hand, dark sunglasses, and my headphones, I was ready to go. There was no use in trying to talk to a tuned-out girl reading a book. Walking to the park for breakfast was not only great exercise, but it was smart to be able to enter and leave a location in any direction I chose. No parked car to have to circle back to. I could enter at one end and exit the park on the other end several miles away, it was large enough that you could undoubtedly lose someone inside.

I ordered the park workers favorite, a number seven off the menu with no changes or substitutions. On any given day, they made dozens of egg, bacon, and cheese sandwiches on a roll. A regular coffee, nothing fancy or different. The less the clerk had to think about my order, the less he thought about me.

I took my boring order to my favorite table by the fountain. This area by the park entrance was the perfect people-watching spot—the ideal place to find my next project. The park was always packed with a fantastic variety of people. There were the basic athletic types of all ages: runners, bike riders, rollerbladers sharing paths with the stroller-pushing moms and nannies. Professional dog walkers came and went from their dog runs. Retired people gathered by chess tables and bocce courts. Families and the younger kids who were learning to ride bikes tended to migrate closer to the playground areas while the teens gathered under the overpasses around the parking lots.

The spot I chose was right at the busiest entrance where most people stopped on their way in or out. It was close enough to the gate that people who worked in town walked over for their lunch breaks. The park deli, as it was known, was a quaint, small, freestanding, refurbished greenhouse with its entrance across from the park's main historical fountain.

The deli had small café tables arranged for its patrons outside, but they weren't a stickler about who sat down and hung around. When there weren't enough seats, many found a place on the fountain ledge or the park's many benches. This day, there were plenty of seats. I was there after the opening rush that consisted of nurses, cops, and construction workers. I had no interest in them. I planned to arrive just before the regular breakfast rush.

On the path that came from a parking lot, I saw him. Even before I could see his face, I knew he was perfect just by the way he carried himself: confident, but not cocky. He walked at a determined but casual pace with a rhythm that implied he could move. He looked a little out of place, wearing an ill-fitting brown corduroy blazer with patches on the elbows and a blue button-down shirt. He had a small gym bag in hand.

Then I saw a woman coming from the opposite direction in yoga pants and four-inch heels. The oddness of their attire was the only thing they had in common. She walked with a juvenile, bouncy skip. Even from a distance, I couldn't miss the big blonde hair. As she got closer, I couldn't help but notice her fake, alien-looking eyes. This woman carried herself in an, "Aren't you lucky to be looking at me? You're welcome," kind of way. As their eyes met, he missed a step and took a deep breath. Pushing his shoulders back, he launched forward with a forced smile.

Oh, this was going to be entertaining.

They kissed on the cheek and walked to the deli entrance together. He had his hands shoved deep in his pockets, and she walked with her hands crossed in front of her chest as if she were cold. Judging by the clerk's body language, I could tell her order was complicated and demanding. She was someone who never wanted to be invisible. Eventually, they came out and looked for a table. I hoped they would choose one close by.

They sat two tables away, directly in my sightline. My lucky day.

I watched as they silently unwrapped their food. It was no surprise that the blonde's order was wrong.

Dismissively, she waved off the offer to go back for her in a huff, "No! I just know they would do something to it!"

Did he? Yes, subtle eye roll. I liked him already.

He offered to give her his food. Oh, no, she didn't want to be a bother. Really, lady? I'd taken on that identity before—the high-maintenance, self-involved, center-of-the-universe type. It was very uncomfortable and exhausting. How do people like that live with themselves?

They settled in, and she was clearly unhappy with her food. He didn't seem overly happy with her, either. They made small talk as they ate. Their interaction had the awkwardness of a blind date, yet an odd intimacy. Intriguing, but I was starting to get bored. Just when I thought I had misjudged the entertainment value of their meeting; he checked his watch and leaned over to whisper something in her ear. She looked horrified.

She launched to her feet, loudly knocking over her chair. This was someone who could never be invisible. Acting the part of a gentleman, he stood up as well. She slapped him in dramatic fashion—indignant, open-palmed, like in a movie. I'm sure all witnesses would probably tell a different version of this morning's show to a friend or a coworker later that day. She briskly walked away, shouting something indignant about his nightly performance, which got a chuckle out of him and the audience. Good sense of humor. No bad feelings on his part; he didn't seem to care in the least. I smiled. Oh, yes, he'd do nicely.

With a gorgeous, genuine, easy smile, he cleaned up the table, throwing away his food and her custom order. He smoothly removed his jacket and shirt, revealing a stylish graphic T-shirt. Tossing the discarded clothing into the gym bag, he sat down and confidently leaned back in his chair. Curious—if he were staying, why would he throw away his breakfast? Was it the heat of the moment? Did he clear the table without thinking? No, Mr. Green Eyes gave every move immense consideration. Did I mention his bright green eyes? Green eyes are the only feature more striking than blue eyes.

He stood, arms wide open, welcoming his next breakfast guest. Pretty brown hair with red highlights in a ponytail. Definitely sporty in her leggings and sneakers. There was something about the way she carried herself as she walked up. Yes, she had to be his sister. She had the same gait. They hugged and laughed as they entered the deli. He said something to the clerk, and they all had a good chuckle. The clerk must have seen the morning's events and noticed the man was ordering again, this time with a different woman.

They returned and sat at the same table, affording me another perfect view. I started to take some mental notes. Confident, stylish, definitely well-off. Were they brand-conscious? They were wearing high-end, brand-name clothing, but his gym bag was a standard no-name bag—something anyone could pick up for a few dollars. Interesting? Or odd? I wasn't sure yet.

Moments later, they were joined by a couple. The guy had platinum-blond hair stylishly slicked back, and clear, almost translucent brown eyes. He had an all-American, guy next door, high school quarterback look to him. An athletic build. A body created by sports, not weights or exercises at a gym. I could see under his trendy button-down shirt his skin had a dark tan. Although he dressed like a country club brat, I could see a playful, laid-back surfer boy under the surface.

The woman who arrived with him also had platinum-blonde hair, but not natural. It had a processed, too perfect tint to it. Her eyes appeared to be a muddy hazel. Or was it brown? Something about the color seemed off. Unnatural? Ah, were those colored contacts? If so, I could teach her a thing or two about fitting in. Little Miss Counterfeit had a self-conscious, low self-esteem, desperate feel about her.

They didn't appear to be a couple. They didn't share any physical chemistry. In fact, she didn't seem very comfortable with him. They had no similar traits, and they barely acknowledged each other as they approached the table. If they were a couple, they were most definitely fighting.

The table got loud with hellos and hugs. Based on these greetings, none of them seemed to be coupled off.

"Where's Tiff?" was met with a round of laughter.

I guessed the high-maintenance blonde was Tiff.

They were a group that took considerable time before leaving the house to make sure every detail was on point. Their clothing looked brand new, perfectly pressed, without a pretentious feel. Even Little Miss Counterfeit was put together well.

This wasn't going to be easy. I could tell the group was tight. It would take a long, slow play. When dealing with a close group of friends, it was essential to identify the leader. Make no mistake—every group had one. It took a trained eye to spot them because they subtly took control. The only thing I could do was wait until something was questioned. The group would naturally look toward the leader for their thoughts. I loved that no one realized it, not even the leader. I'd made the crucial error in the past by choosing the incorrect leader. All that work for nothing. I shook it off. I wouldn't make that mistake again.

Finally, there seemed to be a motion. Maybe a query on what to do next. Everyone in the group voiced their opinions, talking over each other in a way only close friends or family could get away with. There. Ever so slightly, they directed their attention to the sister. She was the only way into the group, and to him.

It was not easy to watch someone closely without looking like a creep. Thankful for the cover my dark glasses and book provide, I focused on her. Did the sister always dress in a sporty casual way, or was she coming from an athletic activity? No, she dressed for the occasion. She was ready for some kind of exercise. She didn't have a bag with her or any equipment. Did she jog? No. Jogging would be inefficient—she ran. It appeared she was watching people come and go on the path. Was she looking for someone? There was a nod of recognition from someone running by. I checked the time. Yes, she ran, and she ran here around this time. Every day? I hoped not; I didn't think I had that in me.

The group didn't stay long. This must have been a meeting point. On their way out of the park, I watched as the duffel bag was handed causally to a homeless man sitting with a cart at the park entrance.

I was tempted to follow, but I didn't want to press my luck. Deciding I had enough information to begin, I gathered myself together and walked home.

Give me a month—maybe two, tops—and I'd be a vital part of their lives.

Chapter 2

After a stroll around the park, I circled back home. It was a beautiful house set far back from the road. No markings—just a narrow dirt driveway framed by cattails and sea oats. The long, wispy, sand-colored stalks swayed in the wind, making a relaxing swishing sound.

Once I passed the threshold of the driveway, my home appeared. From the street, the building looked like an old factory; all brick, with massive industrial-looking windows and a large wooden door. The landscaping around the side was minimal. It seemed more like a parking lot than a front yard. I could fit about fifteen cars outside, four in the garage. That was how I usually entered the house—through the garage. The bright and modern garage currently held two cars. I had a cozy nook where the garage met the house with a bench and places for boots, shoes, and coats. I opened the door and was welcomed by a little security beep. I never had uninvited guests, but it was smart to be prepared.

The sun gleamed off the polished hardwood floors. The back of the house was a stark contrast to the front. Large windows gave way to blue ocean and skies. Nothing to get dreamy eyed and excited over. It was not a functional beach. All rocks and dunes, the easiest way to have a secluded "beachfront" home. The average person wanted a home further down the road with a sandy accessible beach. Most people didn't even know my house was here. Their focus was looking ahead toward the usable beach, uninterested in what lay on this side of the bridge.

Little black book in hand, I retreated to the back patio off the living room. I took a quick glance through my past identities. Sometimes I considered recycling an identity, but I thought this project deserved someone new. I opened a new journal and started to write:

Subjects: Tight group, a brother and sister
(leader); Miss Counterfeit; surfer boy.
No couples. All appear single for now.
Identity: Sporty, sophisticated, laid-back, well-
off, not flaunty.
Name:

Choosing a name was crucial. The emotions
and stigmas attached to some names were staggering.
This time I wanted to be remembered. I wanted them to
hear my name and hold on to it. I wanted them to
remember me. I needed them to remember me. Hannah?
JoAnne? Katherine? Yes! Depending on the group, they
could shorten it to Kathy, Kat, or Kate. It was a likable
name. The last name—now that had to be something
that sounded well-off but not connected to anyone or
anything. It couldn't be hard to pronounce or ethnic
sounding. Consulting Google and random name
generators, I settled on Lindstorm. I looked in the
mirror and smiled. *Hello, nice to meet you, Katherine
Lindstorm.*

Pouring myself a glass of wine, I went out back.
I settled into my oversized Adirondack chair and
breathed in the fresh salt air. I'd start tomorrow. I'd
need my rest.

I woke up early and stretched out in my king-size bed. My mother thought it was ridiculous for one person to have a king-size bed, which was probably the main reason I purchased it. Besides, anything less than a king would look silly. My bedroom was spacious, with large windows and a balcony overlooking the ocean.

Good morning, Katherine Lindstorm! Ready for a run? No, not really. But let's get to it.

This project better be worth it. I pulled my hair into a neat ponytail that accentuated my trendy, natural-looking highlights. I chose a pair of expensive-looking stud earrings, gently worn running shoes, and threw on very fashionable but understated leggings and a coordinated top. I grabbed my new ID and cards fresh off the printer and placed them in their designated slots in my new overpriced phone case. Lastly, I grabbed my AirPods because no one ran without headphones, and I was off.

It took a few days of running—God help me—before crossing paths with my new soon-to-be BFF. After a brief little head nod, I took note of the time, route, and direction. Thankfully, it turned out she was not a daily runner. Three times a week—that was totally doable. I arranged to cross paths in different spots a handful of times over the next two weeks. Often enough that she waved and smiled when we passed. I'd been paying attention. She was always in the same sneakers, but never repeated an outfit. She also never appeared out of breath or sweaty. I was up for the challenge.

One morning, I arranged to be directly in front of her in line at the deli. She came in as I waited for my order. It was timed perfectly. They called out my order: egg white quesadilla with swiss and turkey bacon.

She smiled at me. "That's what I always order."

I smiled back politely and made a comment about it being the best thing on the menu. It was not.

They handed me a vanilla latte with honey.

"With honey? Oh, I'll try that too."

Another comment about it being the best thing ever, which it was. I gave her a friendly smile, "Have a nice day." I left to take a seat outside.

Now, you know it wasn't a coincidence I ordered the same thing as her. I did my homework as Ann. In fact, when I wasn't Katherine, crossing paths with my soon-to-be new BFF, I was Ann. Ann was doing a lot of legwork around town. I couldn't just jump blindly into a project—there was a lot of prep work that went into it. I'd learned quite a bit about Elizabeth and her brother, Adam.

Naturally, I sat close to where she normally did. Not the best view for people watching, but a beautiful view of the fountain. She came over to tell me the honey was an incredible addition to her latte and asked if she could join me.

"Sure, have a seat, I'm just taking a well-deserved break from my run."

"Yes! I think we've crossed paths a few times. I'm Elizabeth—Lizzy for short."

That's right—they had to come to you. It had to be their idea.

"I'm Katherine—Katie for short." I had to match that *e* sound on the end. Subtle familiarities would bring them in closer. And so, the fun began.

It was an art form. Extracting information without seeming eager or nosey. Providing just enough information to be polite and spark interest. The most important part of any first impression: being remembered for the right reasons. Making the person feel something when they talked to me. That feeling would be associated with me and it was hard to undo, so it had to be a good one. I quickly decided Lizzy needed to feel valued, interesting and in control. Not surprised.

As she talked, I nodded in agreement and leaned in. Made her feel like I was giving her my undivided attention. It was important not to talk too long. Needed to avoid that awkward silence. Conversations always had to feel unfinished.

I took the last bite of my sandwich and apologized that I had to get going. "I have to run a few errands uptown and like to get things done early before the crowds."

"Oh, what a coincidence. I was just heading uptown. Were you going to walk?"

"Yes, I was! Are you?"

"Actually, yes. It's not too far, and I find I miss great little shops when I drive."

"Well then, what do you say we take this party on the road, Lizzy? Where do you need to go? I really want to check out that new thrift shop. Such interesting things."

"No way! I love thrift shops! Most of my friends think I'm crazy. Used stuff? Yuck! But I just love the history and thinking about the stories and people behind something as simple as a little hand-painted teapot."

"Exactly! I love the jewelry. Yeah, it's mostly cheap costume jewelry, but most of it is so old and eccentric. You can't find anything like those unique pieces anymore. Everything feels mass-produced. I love finding pretty pieces and remaking them using gold, silver, and real stones. It's what I do, actually."

Lizzy's eyes got big, as I knew they would. "It's fate that has brought us together, Katie. Fate!"

Sure was, Lizzy, sure was.

Chapter 3

"I met a wonderful, genuine person at breakfast. Her name's Katherine Lindstorm. You just have to meet her!" Lizzy called Adam as soon as she got home.

Adam rolled his eyes at his little sister with great exaggeration. "Lizzy, leave me alone. I just got rid of Tiff. I need a break."

Lizzy wasn't about to give up that easy. "She's just your type." Laughing, she couldn't help herself. "The opposite of Tiff"

"Come on, Lizzy, why are you nagging me? If you like her so much, you play her."

"You know, Mom is always looking for you to bring someone around for the holidays. I'm just saying, I think she's your type. You'll like her. Make it a long play, and you won't have to pull someone last minute for the annual Christmas party."

She made a good point. Last year had been a disaster. Adam's last-minute date was not up to par, and things went south fast. While he had found the entire event hysterical, their mother had been mortified. All she asked was that he bring someone she'd be proud to show off. Last year's date had too much to drink and sang raunchy Christmas songs at the bar.

"Come on, Adam, you know she's got to be all that for me to set you up. I've never tried to before, not even after you begged and pleaded when I was in the sorority."

"Okay. Fine, you win. This just might be something worth a look. And why not? With Tiff gone, a new challenge might be fun. Why don't you bring her this weekend to the barbeque? The whole gang can meet your new BFF."

Lizzy was okay with that; she wasn't planning on Katie being temporary. After she met the whole gang, she'd want to stay. Just like Chris did.

Chris was a member of Lizzy's sorority pledge class, and they hit it off right away. If Lizzy was honest, it was Chris's star-struck, passionate desire to be just like her that made her want to take her under her wing. Lizzy was feeling homesick and out of place when Chris bumbled over all big-eyed and introduced herself. She hung on Lizzy's every word, and it was just what she needed. It was expected that Chris would come home with her over the break.

Chris was an only child from an influential family. She was raised by a parade of nannies and sent off to boarding school at the young age of seven. With each nanny and boarding school, Chris tried to fit in. When she saw the confident Lizzy, she was drawn in.

Chris could see Lizzy was alone but knew she wouldn't be for long. Lizzy befriended her while she had the chance—before she gathered followers. Within a month, Lizzy was already an influential member of the sorority. By sophomore year, she was on the executive board, and by her junior year, she was president. When senior year rolled around, she was the national student advisor, and Chris had been by her side the entire way.

Never having had a place to call home, Chris joined Lizzy at her home for every holiday and break. They were inseparable. After graduation, Chris had no plans and no place to go. It seemed natural and logical to follow Lizzy. She was the family Chris never had, and she would do anything to stay a part of the group. She would do anything for them. Anything.

Lizzy was a little worried about how Chris would take to Katie. Even after all these years, she was still so insecure. Truth be told, Lizzy liked her that way. Easy to manipulate. Everyone needed a yes-man. Chris was Lizzy's yes-man. Sometimes she was so much work.

Lizzy sighed. She would have to make sure Chris understood Katie was an addition, not a replacement. They seldom brought new people into the group, and when they did, the game was apparent, and they posed no threat. Katie would be different. Lizzy had it all planned out.

Chapter 4

Yes, I was staring at the phone when Lizzy called. I thought our afternoon was perfect. It rang once. *Can't seem too available. Twice…wait for it…three times—now*!

"Hello? Hi! Yes, it was so much fun. I enjoyed the company. This weekend? I'm not sure; I do have someplace to be in the morning. Sure, send me the information, and I'll try to swing by if it's not too late. Great! See you then."

No, I did not have anything to do that morning, or any morning—oh, except run. I couldn't suddenly disappear from the path. Now that we had connected, Lizzy would be looking for me.

The barbeque started at three. I figured five would be just about right. I needed to be the last one to arrive and give enough time for them to catch up and start talking about the mysterious new guest, Katherine. I could imagine the conversations: *She designs jewelry based on old costume jewelry? Oh, Lizzy, that's such a you thing. You met her where?* The suspense would be killing them. Just when they thought I was a no show, I'd swoop in with a bottle of Caymus Napa Valley Cabernet Savingnon.

Pulling up to the address, I paused. Was this a house or a hotel? My research showed everyone was from affluential families, but damn. My car was valet parked, whether I liked it or not. I didn't. I entered through a black iron side gate down a stone path to the back of the house. The yard was enormous—grossly oversized and groomed. There were easily over a hundred of her "closest friends" there. The pond-shaped pool had flowers floating in it, and there was a tent set up on the grass for those who preferred shade. A commercial-sized bar was built into the deck with what looked like a complete outdoor kitchen, where three uniformed chefs busily completed orders being carried out by waitstaff.

I'd been to weddings that had less than this casual barbeque with close friends. I was wearing a long designer sundress. It fit me perfectly, hugging me in all the right places. I took pride in already owning the dress, although I had a feeling this group would eventually have me scurrying to a store for more appropriate attire. If I was over or underdressed, it was as simple as mentioning I'd come from another event.

I walked in confidently, but not arrogantly— this group would respect no less—and headed directly over to Lizzy. I swiftly passed her brother, who was flashing a big smile. *Oh, I see you, you beautiful man, but I can't give you any attention. Not yet.* Lizzy would appreciate that I didn't notice him, and he'd be intrigued by my lack of interest.

I knew the group was tight and wiggling myself in there would be a challenge. I prepared a couple of funny stories, some comments to toss around, and a few key thoughts to make them feel connected to me. Back to that first-impression rule. As I said, it was essential to bring a feeling. Today that feeling was fun. I wanted them to associate me with fun. "Oh, we should invite Katie. She's fun!" This should become a regular part of the conversation.

I can actually be hilarious. I took on the identity of a stand-up comic for a few months. Now that was fun! It was such a rush standing in front of a room of people and making them laugh at themselves and each other. But that was a different project.

I made sure to spend time talking to everyone—even Adam, although very briefly. I saw him trying to grab my attention several times, but I gave my undivided focus to each person I was speaking to at the moment; this would make them feel very important and interesting. Most people love to feel important and interesting. I made sure to spread my attention around outside the group as well—a regular social butterfly.

Miss Counterfeit, I found out, was Chris. She was nicer than expected, and I almost felt bad for her. She was so unsure of herself and her position in the group. If Adam wasn't so delicious, I might have chosen her for my project. It was easy to see why Lizzy had taken her in, almost like a stray dog, always thankful for any scraps. She was truly a beautiful girl under the superficial facade. She needed a backbone. Maybe I'd try to find time for her. An afternoon out, perhaps. I'd plan an invite for both girls at a time I knew Lizzy wouldn't be able to make it. Hopefully, Lizzy would insist on us going without her, and we'd have some one-on-one time.

Surfer boy was Brandon. I pegged him just right. His parents owned the local country club, but he'd rather spend all his time at the beach surfing. He was smart. He turned his trust fund into an impressive portfolio to prove something to his dad. Now his dad couldn't complain about him spending all his time at the beach instead of in an office.

Adam, dear Adam, I learned very little that I didn't already know because I didn't want to spend much time with him. I needed to leave him feeling like he missed out. No doubt, everyone would be talking about what they learned about Katherine, and he would have nothing to add. He would be hanging on everyone else's every word.

I made my goodbye rounds, ending with Lizzy, giving her the distinct feeling of being the most important person. Something that didn't escape Adam's attention. Apologies for not being able to stay longer. Other commitments, yada yada. Big smiles and hugs. "Yes, let's get together again. I'd love to."

"Did you see that? She barely glanced my way. Maybe she's a lesbian and into Lizzy? That would be an interesting twist." Adam complained.

Brandon rolled his eyes. Brandon had known Adam since kindergarten. They got into a fistfight the very first day of school over who was going to sit next to the pretty teacher at story time. They spent the day in the principal's office waiting for their parents and had been the best of friends ever since.

"Adam, not every female on the planet wants you."

"Don't be a hater, Brandon. I noticed she didn't look at you either."

"Is that a challenge, Adam?" Brandon had no interest in Lizzy's new BFF, but he wasn't going to let Adam know that. "Maybe you failed to notice we had a very nice extensive conversation."

"No, I think I'm just going to have to call dibs on this one."

"What is this? Seventh grade? She's all yours, Adam—good luck. I think you're going to need it." Brandon couldn't stop the song Maneater from playing in his head and laughed.

Brandon and Adam rejoined the group, all talking at once about Katherine until Lizzy took control. "See, I told you! She's wonderful!"

"Not that I would know. I didn't get to talk to her. You guys were all over her like sharks on fresh meat," Adam complained.

Lizzy rolled her eyes. On her cue, Chris followed suit. Chris always followed Lizzy's lead blindly. Was something funny? Not unless Lizzy thought so. Chris was very thankful Lizzy liked Katie. Katie made Chris feel important, like her opinion mattered.

Brandon chimed in that she seemed chill and thought she could hang. He was a little uncomfortable with how easy it was to open up with her. Next time, he would make an effort to muddy that—throw in a fib here and there, put up a little wall.

Everyone seemed to be on board with Katie. Lizzy was pleased.

Chapter 5

It was a couple of days before Lizzy and I crossed paths again. Interestingly, she wasn't running alone. Adam, with his long strides, was speed walking to Lizzy's run. I could see the competitiveness between them. Lizzy would never concede and would rather pass out than admit it was challenging to keep up with him. She was even breaking a sweat, something I knew she didn't enjoy. Adam was obviously not a runner. He looked hot and tired but actively tried to seem cool. Like Lizzy, he would never slow his pace. They both look relieved to see me. Finally, they got to stop the facade of running.

I feel you—enough with the running.

"Hi, Adam! Funny seeing you here. I didn't know you ran." *Obviously, you don't.* Big smile at Lizzy—*yes, Lizzy, I see what's going on.* I watched as Adam attempted to catch his breath.

"No, actually, I don't. I thought I'd keep my sister company today on the off chance of running into you."

I was not expecting that forwardness, and it almost threw me off—especially with those eyes. Almost.

"Aren't you lucky? 'Cause here I am! Have you guys had breakfast?"

They both looked relieved to not have to run another second, and we walked to the deli. I let Lizzy go on to Adam about our fateful first meeting and how she now had to have honey in her latte. Adam rolled his eyes and reminded her he'd already heard the story several times. Lizzy was mortified, and her ego needed a quick rescue.

"Well, I'm sure you weren't listening the first few times. Besides, stories of fateful meetings such as ours should be told over and over," I said.

That did it. Lizzy was in the pocket. In her eyes, I could do no wrong. In one sentence, I had just become the best friend she had ever had and the only friend she would ever need.

While we ate our breakfast, there was small talk and not a lot of new information. Suddenly, Adam and Lizzy started talking faster. It seemed like random topics all being spoken about at the same time with them taking turns asking me questions or my opinion. I was having a little trouble following along. Almost felt like an interrogation.

Abruptly, I stood and apologized, "I'm sorry I need to get home to walk the dog." Why did I say that? It was the first thing that popped into my head. I didn't have a dog. I didn't want a dog. Now I had to go out and get a dog. Wondered if I could rent one. You could rent almost anything these days.

It turns out you couldn't rent a dog, but you could foster one. Unfortunately, there were all sorts of background checks and waiting periods. I think getting a gun might be more accessible. Actually, I knew it was. The way his eyes lit up when I said I had a dog. I had no other choice. I went online and consulted my good friend, Google. I gathered information about adopting versus buying a dog, the different breeds of dogs, and how to train and take care of a dog.

Considering this dog was expected to already be part of my life, I needed to adopt a dog that was already trained. Since I didn't know if any of the friends had allergies, I needed to go with a hypoallergenic dog. What the heck made them hypoallergenic? I hoped they weren't bald like the hypoallergenic cats I'd seen on social media.

At the pound, there was a sweet, white—I think she was white—Bichon Frise–poodle mix. Thankfully, I learned hypoallergenic dogs have hair, not fur. Fine by me. I was glad they didn't look like shaved cats. I took her directly to the groomer, who wanted to know her name and what happened to the poor baby.

"She's a rescue. Poor thing was found wandering the streets." I looked down at her big brown eyes under dirty, matted hair. *You're gonna need a name.* Out of the corner of my eye, I spotted a bright ruby-red collar and leash set, part of a *Wizard of Oz* outfit. "Her name is Ruby." Sounded good to me. Ruby seemed to like her new name, jumping at the sound of it, tail wagging.

I left the newly named Ruby in the capable hands of Pete and his staff. He warned me she may need to be shaved if they were unable to brush all the knots out, but that would be a last resort. I guessed I could make up a story about her getting something gross in her hair, requiring a shave. I'd cross that bridge if it came to that.

I walked to the library to do some more research on all things dog. I never had a pet, nor had I ever wanted one, not even as a child. My family traveled all over the country, and later, the world as my mom's fame grew. Her self-help books were published internationally in several languages. We were a busy, happy family. I didn't feel like we were missing out on anything by not having pets.

Two hours later, I received a text that Ruby was ready to be picked up. Pete and the staff were very excited and proud to present Ruby with a full body of freshly washed, soft white hair. They went on and on telling me how good she was. "We had to wash her three times! Can you imagine?"

I guess that wasn't the norm. I thanked them profusely and sounded as happy and excited as I could, tipping what I assumed was more than enough for all the work that went into saving her hair.

I got the *Wizard of Oz*-themed ruby-red collar and matching leash. It seemed only fitting. Much to the groomer's dismay and objection, I decided against the coordinated Dorothy outfit. Really, who would dress a dog? Psychopaths, that was who. Besides, I couldn't imagine a grown man being in favor of that concept—

except for the groomer, obviously. Ruby did clean up nicely if I said so myself. I was sure everyone would fall madly in love with her. I hoped the slip wasn't a mistake. It would be tragic if the project ended abruptly due to a dog. I looked down at her wagging tail and flopping tongue and smiled. I might keep her around, regardless. We'd see.

Thank God I acted on that dog slipup fast. Adam texted that same night, asking all about my dog—name, breed, and how about a picture? I sent a picture of Ruby strategically on my lap with my legs stretched out, crossed at my ankles. He asked if he could join me for a walk with her in the park instead of my run.

Oh, I love you, Ruby! Good job, girl!

Chapter 6

"Adam, I told you she was amazing! She even has a dog! You're a sucker for dogs." Adam smiled at Lizzy. She was right. He really did have a soft spot for dogs, and once even stayed in a relationship longer to spend time with a girl's Siberian husky.

When Adam was seven, his mom brought home a golden retriever. He was a large, hairy, beautiful creature, and Adam fell immediately in love.

Adam's mom was at a luncheon one afternoon when the conversation and everyone's attention was hijacked by a woman in the group and talk of her new puppy. Adam's mom needed to regain control of the conversation. She knew a puppy didn't have a chance at the mention of a golden retriever rescued from a hurricane down south. The unfortunate thing had been through so much.

Later that week, when that group came to the house for a book club meeting, the dog needed to be present. No one needed to know the dog was purchased from a pet store. After that group was no longer a part of Adam's mom's life, the dog suddenly disappeared.

Adam was devastated. He never learned what happened and could only hope his mother found a loving home for him. They never had a pet after that. His mom learned her lesson. She was not a fan of a big, hairy creature underfoot, drooling all over the house.

"I wonder what kind of dog." Lizzy didn't know, and she didn't like that.

"It's a little white fluffy dog, maybe a Maltese mix. Here, look. I have a picture."

Lizzy snatched the phone from Adam, she hated the smug look on his face "How do you have a picture?"

"I don't need to inform you of all my communications. I'm seeing her and Ruby tomorrow."

"Tomorrow? Shit you move fast. We just saw her this morning." Lizzy whined; she didn't like feeling out of the loop.

"It's not a date. Just a walk in the park with Ruby, her dog." The dog was a great excuse. He saw the opening and took it. Ruby was a dainty little thing, very cute. He loved the picture Katherine had sent. He couldn't take his eyes off the legs in the photo—very distracting. "I'll call you after, Lizzy. Fill you in."

Adam left Lizzy stewing in the living room. How had she not known her new BFF had a dog? Lizzy tried to put these feelings aside. She'd know everything about her dearest Katie. It would take time. She'd need to do it before Adam got the chance. BFF trumped soulmate. It would be important, should anything happen between the two of them, that the relationship with Lizzy was strong enough to never waver. Lizzy needed Katie to come to her with any problems between the two of them so she could smooth things over. Lizzy could see it now—holidays, vacations, Sunday dinners. Katie would not only be her BFF, but the sister she always wanted. In her mind, she was already Aunt Lizzy.

Chapter 7

I arrived at the park deli later than planned.
Typically, I liked to make an entrance, but I wasn't
counting on Ruby stopping at every damn tree. Each
time I thought that little bladder couldn't possibly hold
another drop, she stopped again.

I saw him, but I didn't acknowledge him. I
wanted him to think he had the upper hand, seeing me
first and watching me walk down the road. He waved me
over—so cute and eager. I made eye contact and smiled.
With a casual little kiss on the cheek, he handed me a
vanilla latte with honey and placed a small bowl of water
on the ground for Ruby. *Very thoughtful and sweet.*

I knew which topics would keep Adam talking, preventing him from asking too many questions. It was a beautiful day. Everything was going as planned. I was relaxed, enjoying our time together, until I saw someone out of the corner of my eye who I vaguely remembered from an old project. Oh crap. It had only been a year, but many identities ago. I turned my back to the road and bent down to give Ruby some attention. I hoped he'd walk right by, missing me entirely.

"Matt! Come meet Katherine."

Matt's big smile quickly vanished when our eyes met, but he managed to shake my hand and introduce himself. Adam was talking a mile a minute, explaining how Matt had missed getting to meet me at the barbeque.

So, this is the last member of the group.

In conversation, they referenced the group in fives—*the five of us went here; the five of us did this*. I assumed the fifth member was the now-exiled Tiff. Should have known better. She didn't quite fit.

Adam was oblivious to Matt's awkwardness and insisted he sit with us. Reluctantly, he agreed. "I guess— if you're sure. Let me grab a coffee."

"You have a coffee in your hand."

"What? Oh yeah, it's cold. I'm gonna get a new one. Be right back."

Matt tossed his coffee into the trash as he walked into the deli. I saw him staring at me through the glass. I made a conscious effort to not make eye contact.

"I hope you don't mind. Matt's had a tough year. If I run into him, I try to keep him out as long as I can."

"Of course, no problem. He seems nice. How do you know him?" Adam seemed genuinely concerned for Matt, which was another sweet little gesture.

"We go way back. You know Brandon? Matt was Brandon's RA freshman year of college. We thought he was a real hard-ass until we ran into him wasted at a party and found out he was only three months older than us." He laughed at the memory. "Let's just say we bailed him out that night, and we've been tight ever since."

Matt returned and sat down. There was a bit of an awkward pause as Adam reached his arm over, rather possessively, and rested it on the back of my chair—laying claim, no doubt. Adam attempted to continue the story of the fateful night they met, but Matt interrupted him. "I'm sorry, you look just like someone I know. It's uncanny. I'd bet my life you were her."

Thankfully, I was a quick thinker and smooth talker. *Never let them see you sweat or even twitch.* My mom had taught me well. I don't miss a beat. I smiled and let out a fun, flirtatious laugh. "Well, I hope it's someone enticing!"

That's right, Adam. I'm not going to be that easy.

Matt visibly shook the thought from his head, smiled back, and laughed along with me. His laugh sparked a memory. I was Jennifer when I met him. Blond with brown eyes—always wearing stylish but studious glasses. Jennifer was very casual, laid back, and smart. We had a lot of fun together—a lot of laughs. Did I meet any of his friends or family? How messy was this going to get? I'd need to check that journal as soon as I got home.

My phone rang on schedule. No one was on the other end. It was an automated message I had made. A friend needed a ride. It was a preplanned excuse to leave "I'm sorry to cut our lunch short." Lunch, not date.

"Maybe I can keep you company on the drive." I saw Adam wasn't ready to give up on today, and he was quick to bail on Matt.

"That's so nice of you, but it's a personal thing. I don't think she would want a stranger along for the ride. I'm sure you understand." I ran off abruptly. I didn't want to get too close to Adam too quickly. Besides, I really wanted to get home to see if Matt was going to be a problem.

***

"I don't know. Something doesn't seem right. She looks so much like Jennifer! I wish I had a photo," Matt said.

Adam rolled his eyes.

Matt had gone off the deep end after Jennifer ghosted him. Matt's friends never met the elusive Jennifer. She was in and out of his life like a tornado, leaving him in shambles.

Matt had left Adam a message saying he had finally met "the one." After Matt was a no show for an event, Adam went to his apartment to find him living in squalor. He credited himself for *saving* Matt, convincing him to get up, shower, dress, and leave the house. He even had his maid come over and clean the place up. Naturally, Matt was billed. It wasn't like someone died.

"Your Jennifer is nothing like my Katherine," Adam snapped.

Matt gave this some serious thought, then nodded in agreement. "I think the Yankees are playing. Let's head over to the club. Brandon is probably there. We can catch the game together."

The mention of baseball and the club instantly changed Adam's mood. "Great idea. Let's go."

Later that night, alone and a little drunk from the free-flowing seven and seven at the club, Adam couldn't stop thinking about the moment he first saw Katherine. She was unlike anyone he had ever met. He had never seen someone walk into a gathering with such confidence. She worked the room like an expert.

He didn't take her for a dog person. In fact, every now and then he got a vibe off her that didn't seem to fit. Adam was intrigued. Staring at the photo she sent, he thought, *She's like reading a mystery novel with a twist on every page. A book you pick up and can't put down. And those legs—damn!*

The group's monthly game night was coming up, and no one left until the game was finished. Adam needed Lizzy to invite Katherine. She wouldn't be able to run off. An entire night together would be the perfect opportunity to make some progress.

"Hey Lizzy, are we all set for game night?"

Lizzy always had at least six months' worth of games in different planning stages. She lived for it, and Adam knew it.

"Almost. Just some final touches."

"Have I ever told you how much I appreciate all the work you put into game night? You've been putting these together for what—two years now?"

"Three—three years."

Lizzy knew Adam was up to something.

"How many people are coming? Just wondering if you included Matt or not."

"I'm planning on him being here, but I have a plan B if he's a no-show. Why wouldn't he come? What aren't you telling me?" Lizzy asked curtly.

Adam heard the panic sneaking into her voice. He figured she expected Matt at game night. But he was the only one who ever missed a game night, which sent the night into disarray. Since then, Lizzy had been on edge and always planned for his absence, just in case.

Adam gave a final, gentle nudge. He couldn't have her crack under pressure; that wouldn't help. "OK, I was just thinking. Do you have an odd or even number of players? An odd number of players always works better, especially splitting up into groups."

Lizzy sighed. "What if we invite Katherine? I think I can rework everything."

"That's a great idea. That girl, Jo, always has trouble playing. Katherine can pick up her slack." Adam never liked Jo and wanted to cement the invite.

"Oh God, yes, she's a disaster. Katherine must come. Why didn't I think of it sooner? Let's see if Katherine has game."

Adam smiled as he listened to her ramble on, he could still play his sister after all these years.

Chapter 8

My office was a pretty room with curved walls and bookshelves, a fireplace, and a wall of windows overlooking the ocean. When I had designed the room, I imagined myself working in this office, but it turned out I couldn't think in the space. I could count on one hand the number of times I had sat at my pine desk.

Every project had its own journal. The bookshelves were lined with them, each with nothing but a code on the spine for my reference. Choosing Jennifer Wrede's journal off the bookshelf, I started flipping through the pages. My memory wasn't great when it came to Jennifer. She was a quick project, and Matt didn't even know the target. By the look on his face, I thought I had forgotten something crucial.

As I read, I remembered Jennifer needed a friend to be seen with in public, he was a convenient cover. *Nice guy*. I was so preoccupied with the actual target; I didn't notice Matt falling in love with Jennifer. He was simply unfortunate collateral damage.

Anxiously pacing back and forth, I started talking to myself. "I can't believe Matt is part of this group. How did I miss that important little tidbit? It doesn't matter. I would have taken on Adam anyway. He's too delicious to pass up."

Ruby stared at me as if she understood what I was saying.

Am I talking to dogs now?

Lizzy's call startled me back to reality. I shook my head and sat down. Ruby was quick to assume her spot next to me, her head on my lap. I could feel the desperation and stress in Lizzy's voice, and agreed right away with little information.

What the heck was game night? They didn't seem like the kind of group that would have a game night. Were they drinking games? No, they weren't the get drunk types, which was a shame. Drinkers were so easy to work. Once drunk, they told me all sorts of stuff and then didn't remember what they divulged. Really, nothing made a project more manageable than a drinker or two in the group. Board games? That would be too ordinary. The anticipation was killing me.

I slipped into black jeans and a cute black shirt—nothing too fancy. Fun blue suede pumps would help dress up the outfit if needed. If the game night was a casual event, I could always kick them off and go barefoot. I made sure to accessorize with some of my "custom" jewelry. I never purchased jewelry from a thrift shop or refurbished anything. Instead, I got it all online; it was all fake. Vintage reproductions with glass stones and shiny metals—inexpensive but real looking enough. They saw what they wanted to see. It was all part of the show.

I arrived precisely on time. Since I didn't really know what was going on, I couldn't be late. Lizzy and Adam both opened the door. I had a feeling they were both trying to be the one to greet me. I made a point of acknowledging Lizzy first. *Throw him off and let her think she has the power.*

Lizzy handed me an envelope and a box.

"Go take these to the guest room—the last door on the right." She pointed down a long hallway of doors toward the assigned guest room. "Take your time. Not everyone is here. I have to change."

The guest room looked like an upscale hotel room, complete with its own full bath and minibar. The card in the envelope simply read:

> Dear Player,
> Welcome to game night.
> This evening, you will be playing the part of Scarlet. The year is 1923.
> All will be revealed as the evening and game progresses. Stay in character until the game is completed. Be sure to read all notes privately and thoroughly.
> Be careful what you reveal and to whom.

This was a game I was pretty sure I'd kill at. I needed to play Scarlet as Katherine would. An identity taking on an identity—this was new. I had to be careful not to do or say anything that would remotely remind Matt of Jennifer. Fortunately, Jennifer and Katherine were very different identities.

There was a handwritten note attached to the top of the box:

Katie,

I guessed your size. If it doesn't fit, hit "2" on the house phone, and we can raid my closet for something else. You're gonna have a great time— just go with it!

XOXO,

Lizzy

The box contained a gorgeous white-and-silver beaded 1920s evening gown. It was a perfect fit. There were even long white gloves and a rhinestone headband to go with it. The dress was cut very low in the front and back. It would not have been my choice, or Katherine's, but I could pull it off. I wondered, *Is this a test? Is Lizzy testing my willingness to follow her lead? Testing my modesty? Maybe testing her brother's self-control?*

My jewelry matched perfectly. I wasn't sure the blue shoes went with the 1920s theme, but they looked good with the dress. I fashioned my hair up into a loose knot, which complimented the headband and made the neckline appear more dramatic.

Adam practically hit the floor as I walked into the dining room, and Lizzy let out a happy squeal.

Everyone looked fantastic in their 1920s-inspired formal wear, especially Adam. Holy tuxedo. My heart skipped a beat, and my stomach did a little flip. He even had that gorgeous thick hair of his slicked to the side. I felt like I had walked on to the set of *The Great Gatsby*, with Adam as the lead. I counted fifteen players, including me, in attendance.

The game was fun, and I was good at it. I made a conscious effort to slip up from time to time. The food was terrific, served by staff also dressed for the time period. With each course, everyone was handed a single envelope labeled "For Your Eyes Only," which contained instructions to carry out or information for their use. It was fun to watch everyone try to take on their characters. At first, it was challenging to figure out who people were supposed to be or what they were trying to say.

After a few drinks, Jo, one of the girls in the group, said, "I give up! My envelope says I need to let you know that…"

Everyone laughed, and I took note: Jo liked to drink. That could come in handy. Adam, on the other hand, slid into character with ease and played it well.

We ran around the house playing out weird scenarios and looking for clues. I found myself alone with Adam earlier in the evening than planned, but I

went with it. My heel caught on the rug. Down I went—
better catch me! Thankfully, he did. We were close
enough that I could smell rum on his warm breath. I
knew he could smell my perfume—light, fresh, and
clean.

Our eyes met as I glanced at his smile. "Thanks
for the assist," I whispered. I slowly moved away and
grabbed the item we were looking for. "Found it!" I
yelled, drawing the party into the room. Not so fast,
Adam. I needed to build anticipation.

For the rest of the party, I made a point of
spending time with each person, getting to know them
all better. I didn't want any opportunities with Adam
again too soon. This project would only work if we were
a group before we were a couple.

Disappointingly, Jo turned out to be a dead end.
She wasn't a crucial part of the group—an acquaintance
who liked to party and not much else. Everything she
said made little to no sense. In fact, most people in
attendance outside of the core group seemed like extras
in a movie. No real connections—all distant
acquaintances.

I could see Adam working behind me, trying to
casually catch up. It looked like Brandon was following
Lizzy around the same way. Interesting. I needed to
explore that some more. Lizzy, being so self-involved,

was entirely unaware. *Let's see*, I thought, *anyone else with a crush?* I laughed to myself—so many games were going on at once.

Once the game was finished, I made my rounds of goodbyes. As always, I ended with Lizzy, making vague plans to meet for lunch soon.

***

The day after game night, Adam paced back and forth in the spacious white-on-white kitchen his mom had designed to her exact specifications. It had been featured in a home décor magazine. The cover photo taken of her in the room was the last time she set foot in it. Not long afterward, on the day Lizzy turned eighteen, their mother retired from her job as a stay-at-home mom and promptly moved out to the summerhouse. Almost immediately after, their father moved into a city apartment closer to work and further from his wife.

Adam resorted to talking to himself. "I can do this. I can. Damn, this woman throws me off my game. I had the opportunity, and I hesitated. Why did I hesitate? I know, control. I feel like I may lose all control, and I like being in control."

He couldn't stop thinking about Katherine and the moment they shared. This was new for Adam; he always had the upper hand. With Katherine, he was pretty sure he didn't. Continuing his conversation with himself, he opened his laptop and picked up his coffee mug. "I need more information. I think it's time for a chance meeting. How am I now just realizing I don't know where she lives? I can't even stake out her house. Time to call in some favors and get a background check. I need to be the one in control, and somehow, I don't think I am."

Adam was hunched over his laptop, sitting at the kitchen island feverishly typing and talking to himself. He was so involved in his research he didn't even notice Lizzy come and go. She was delighted with herself.

It took Adam quite a bit of time and money to find Katherine's home address, business name, net worth, and date of birth. Everything he needed and then some. He looked up and realized the entire day had passed while he worked.

There was a note from his sister: "Take it easy there, tiger. Don't forget to eat something."

A PB and J sat waiting on a plate. He snatched it up and went to shower and dress. *Now it begins*, he thought. *Now it begins*.

Adam drove down an upscale street lined with beautiful, refurbished homes, looking for Katherine's address. He hadn't imagined her living in a neighborhood like this and thought he had the wrong address when he spotted Katherine reading a book and drinking coffee on a porch. She looked radiant with the sun gleaming off her hair. Ruby was asleep at her feet. They both looked relaxed, enjoying a peaceful afternoon. He wasn't expecting to see her, and for a moment, he was tempted to stop. Adam knew better, a chance visit would need to wait until all his ducks were in a row, and he knew everything he needed to about Katherine. First things first, he needed to roll up his sleeves and finish gathering information.

What makes her tick? Likes? Dislikes?

He'd been playing these games for a long time, and he was good at them. Tiff was fun, but easy. Katherine—now there was a challenge. Katherine made for a great game.

***

Lizzy decided Adam needed a little help and chose a quiet place for lunch with Katherine. A place where she could slip the bartender a hundred-dollar bill and he'd know to serve Lizzy with a light hand and her guest a double. By the end of the day, Lizzy planned to know everything Adam needed to get close to Katherine.

Lizzy let Adam think Katherine was just another game. She wasn't. No more games. She liked Katherine and felt it was time for the group to stop playing and settle down. She thought Matt would be first, but Jennifer had burned him hard. She thought he might remain single forever. Chris wasn't allowed to find someone. She had to be last, and Lizzy wanted to handpick that addition. Adam had to be first. After Adam was in a relationship, Brandon would follow, and Lizzy would be waiting for him.

Chapter 9

Modern technology had its perks. Creating a proper identity with a complete background that could withstand security checks used to take months. Now, in a single day, I could create a kick-ass identity with a digital footprint going back five years. Thanks to security paranoia, anyone could receive notifications when background checks were run. My phone had been buzzing all morning. It looked like someone was finally checking out Katherine.

I packed a small bag and headed over to the address on Katherine's record. It was a beautiful light-blue Victorian home that I started house sitting a month ago. Ruby and I settled in quickly and went about our typical day.

Ruby loved the sun on the front porch, and I decided to take advantage of the rocking chair. I wanted to be visible for my little inquisitive friend. Coffee in one hand and a novel in the other, I got comfortable. Designer sunglasses saved me from the sun's afternoon glare and hid my eyes. It looked like I was reading, but through my sunglasses I watched the street for familiar or slow-moving cars. It wasn't long before I spotted Adam. He thought he was so slick, casually driving by, pretending not to see me. I knew he had and thought, *What's your next move, lover boy?*

Rocking on the front porch was peaceful and mundane. I liked it. I stayed outside until the sun set and the bugs forced us inside.

The next day, I had lunch with Lizzy. I wondered if she knew he drove by. How involved was she in this?

She picked the restaurant, and I was happy to see it was a small, casual, quiet place. She insisted on meeting there, and she was already seated when I arrived five minutes early.

So much for checking it out in advance.

I could tell my Negroni was unusually strong. After a while I casually asked to try Lizzy's Martini. As expected, it was very light. I wasn't even sure there was alcohol in hers.

Dihydromyricetin—*Hovenia dulcis* extract—is a dietary supplement that helps protect the liver and brain from alcohol, and it reduced feelings of intoxication. My mother had my sister and I take it every day. I had never been drunk a day in my life, nor have I ever had a hangover. Staying in control was very important. Drunks were entertaining, but I often felt very embarrassed for them.

Game on, Lizzy. I can play drunk. What do you want to know?

It was clear Lizzy and I had the same objective: getting Adam on the hook. But she wanted me on his hook. I fed her some information and wondered if he knew she was here on his behalf. She felt comfortable and secure.

Let's see what I can find out.

"Brandon is cute. What's his story?"

Ah yes, there it is—a little sparkle in the eye. So, the admiration does go both ways. Lizzy launched into a monologue of adoration. It seemed like these two needed a little push. With a slight blush, Lizzy caught herself and launched into a personal pitch for Adam.

Don't worry, Lizzy. Brandon is all yours.

Lunch was fun. I could see myself being friends with Lizzy. She had a soft, caring side for her brother and would do anything for him, which was all the more reason to get her preoccupied. She needed to focus on Brandon, not me.

We overheard a couple at the bar talking about their hike to a waterfall that afternoon. Lizzy got so excited she almost knocked her drink over. "Wow! That sounds so nice, doesn't it? We should go on Friday! It would be so much fun!"

Hiking? Sure, why the heck not? At least it's not running. I knew the trail. When I was Debbie, my project took me hiking every week. It could be so peaceful. What I remembered most from this trail was the fork. If I could get Brandon and Lizzy to turn right, I'd go left. They'd find themselves in the most beautiful spot, where sunrays touch the top of a wildflower field. If I could plant enough seeds in their minds and get them alone, it might be the perfect romantic setting to tip the scale.

We made plans to go for a hike on Friday. Short notice, but I was up for the challenge. The next day, I got to work.

"Hi, Brandon, funny seeing you here!" Not really funny—it was very planned.

Brandon had told me about the coffee at this café after Lizzy mentioned I was a regular coffee virtuoso with my honey secret. I'd been loitering around waiting on him all morning.

I explained I was in the neighborhood checking out the boutiques when I saw the café and remembered what he said. "After your rave reviews, I couldn't pass up the chance to try their latte. Hey, have you ever hiked the northern trail to the waterfall? I was thinking of heading up there tomorrow. You like photography, right? There are some great spots."

I could see him thinking. He was hesitating; he didn't want to step on Adam's toes.   "Yeah, Lizzy and I were talking about going up if the weather holds. The more the merrier—that is, unless you have other plans. I know it's short notice."

That's right; Lizzy was going. I had his interest now.

"Yeah, sure. I don't really have any plans, and it's going to be nice out."

"Lizzy was telling me how you all grew up together. I said you must be like a brother to her." There it was—he'd gone a little pale. "But she was quick to correct me. Lizzy made it clear you were definitely not like a brother."

"What do you mean? What did she say?"

I heard a touch of eagerness in his voice. I brushed it off. "Nothing, really. Just that she doesn't think of you as a brother."

I could see the wheels turning, but he managed a cool response. "See you on Friday. Eight a.m.?"

***

Brandon wandered around the mall helplessly. *Hiking? Photography? Crap, I don't remember saying that. I must have had too much to drink. Now I have to go get hiking stuff and a camera.*

Focusing on the hiking and photography did little to help keep his mind off what Katherine said. He definitely didn't think of Lizzy as a sister, so why was the idea of her not thinking of him like a brother consuming his thoughts?

***

Lizzy called Adam, "Katie and I are going for a hike to a waterfall—a waterfall!"

"Ok Lizzy, have fun."

"Listen, I have no idea how far it is, but I'll need to rest my feet at just the right moment, and you two go ahead to the bottom of the falls."

"Wait, this is a set up?"

"Yes, now you get it. Seriously, do you think I'd go hiking if it weren't for a game?"

"Fine, I'm going to stop at the sporting goods store while I'm out. Do you need me to bring anything home?"

"I guess whatever you pick up for yourself, buy me a version." Lizzy looked in her closet and sighed. "What the heck do you wear to hike?"

"I'll take care of it. It's the least I can do. I appreciate the assistance with Katherine."

"Yeah, sure. You owe me," Lizzy said.

Adam hung up the phone. He shook his head. *Hiking? I don't know what one wears to hike. This athletic, outdoorsy thing is getting exhausting.*

He was starting to miss Tiff and her lounging around.

Thanks to the knowledgeable staff and his unlimited credit limit, he and Lizzy would be dressed and ready. Returning home, he handed Lizzy her share of packages and retired to his room to research hiking. By the next morning, he knew the trail map forward and backward. Determined to sweep Katie off her feet, Adam packed everything they might need and then some. He was going to be prepared.

Chapter 10

We met in the parking lot. I was not expecting
Lizzy to bring a plus-one. "Hi, Adam, I didn't know you
were coming."

Lizzy threw me a sly smile.

OK, back at ya, Lizzy. I smiled. Looking over
her shoulder, I waved. "Brandon! Glad you could make
it!"

The look on Lizzy's face was priceless.

Looking at the group, I had to laugh. They all
had brand-new hiking boots. *Oh boy, their feet are going
to hurt! You got to break those babies in before hiking
all day.*

No one had a bag—no water, no snacks, no toilet paper.

"Great day for a hike! Before we go, does anyone need to hit the store for water? The bathroom?"

Oh, they were all a little green. Lizzy went pale at the mention of the bathroom.

"Let me grab my gear," Adam said, running back to his car.

I could see him at the trunk, pulling out a massive backpack with a metal frame—the kind someone would pack for a weekend trip, not a day hike. It was clearly brand new—clean, stiff, and shiny. Returning, he smugly announced, "I'm all set. I hope everyone likes white wine and chicken salad."

No need to fake any enthusiasm; I loved chicken salad. "Great, Adam! I have fruit, cheese, and water. Everyone ready?"

It's OK; this will work.

A foursome was easy to operate. No one felt like a third wheel. Same plan: I'd twist my ankle. Adam would stay back with me, and I'd insist Lizzy and Brandon continue ahead to the view. Once there, it was really up to them. Hopefully, I could get them turned around and a little lost together. I'd direct them down to the dead end. It would take them thirty minutes or so, more if they took time to appreciate it.

The trail wasn't an easy one—lots of rocks and tree roots to climb around. Just before the designated fork in the path, I fell into Adam. *Another good catch.*

I sat on a large rock at the side of the road just next to the stream. Adam sat next to me. Holding my ankle, he slowly removed my boot. *Such a gentle touch.* I felt it everywhere. *Keep it together.*

"Ankle looks fine, but you should rest. I'll stay here with you."

"Thanks, it's just a little sore. Lizzy, why don't you and Brandon go ahead? Keep going straight and take the first marked left. Make sure you take lots of pictures at the end of the path. I can't wait to see them!"

If you can figure out how to use the camera. Based on the way he was holding it the boy had no clue.

Adam turned toward me with an adorable smirk. "Isn't that path just a long dead end?"

How did he know that? He probably thought I orchestrated the entire thing to be alone with him. He was partially correct.

"How about some of your wine and my cheese while we rest?" *Let's loosen up, shall we?*

***

Lizzy and Brandon followed Katherine's directions. The trail was narrow, with dense vegetation on both sides. There were no other hikers anywhere, and the path seemed endless. Lizzy and Brandon rarely spent time alone. They walked in awkward silence until they came to what looked like a dead end. Pushing an overgrown branch aside, Brandon revealed a clearing as big as a football field filled with wildflowers.

Lizzy stopped dead in her tracks. "Oh my God! This is…this is—"

"Amazing."

"Yes!" Lizzy started laughing as she spun around with her arms out in a *Sound of Music* way. "To think I was going to suggest turning back!"

Taken with the sight of Lizzy in the field, he started snapping pictures.

"Brandon, what's with the camera?" Lizzy asked.

He shook his head in an adorable, boyish way. "I don't know. I must have said something about taking pictures to Katie, and it stuck with her."

Lizzy laughed. "You know better than that. Never drop a detail you aren't ready to follow up. It's not like you're new to this."

He laughed back. "I know. I must have been distracted."

"Does she distract you?"

"No, you do. You distract me."

Lizzy felt like time stood still as he walked toward her. In the blink of an eye, he swooped in and grabbed her in a forceful but gentle way—the side of her head with one hand, her hip with the other. The kiss was sudden and unexpected. Her legs went weak as she leaned into him.

He slowly pulled away, looked her in the eyes, and smiled. "I've been waiting a long time to do that. I'm sorry; I couldn't help myself."

"Don't wait so long next time, and I'll forgive you." Lizzy smiled. "Let's take more pictures with that camera of yours to show Katie."

Brandon and Lizzy were gone for at least an hour. They walked the path back, holding hands, laughing, and chatting. They subtly dropped hands as they approached Adam and Katherine.

Brandon did a bit of whispering, and Lizzy was blushing. Adam and Katherine both noticed.

"What's up with you?" Adam asked Brandon. "You look like a toddler caught with his hand in the cookie jar."

"I'm sure I don't know what you mean," Brandon said, raising an eyebrow and glancing down at the ankle in Adam's hands.

"There's no waterfall, but Brandon and I got great pictures of wildflowers."

"Waterfall? I never said it was down that road. I thought you'd like the flowers. Come on. The waterfall is this way. My ankle feels better. Follow me." Retrieving her foot from Adam, Katherine put her sock and boot back on.

Adam took Katherine's hand to help her up and held on to it. He smiled. "To help with your balance."

The group made their way down a rocky path to the bottom of the falls. Laying out a blanket, they all sat to relax and eat the sandwiches Adam had packed. The chicken salad was on point.

"Did you make this, Adam?" Katherine asked.

"Yes," he replied smugly.

Lizzy almost spat out her food.

"Well, it's delicious. What's in it?" Katherine asked.

"Yes, Adam, do tell. What's in it?" Lizzy chimed in with a smirk.

Adam looked over at Lizzy, and in a perfect French accent he said, "First, I started with rotisserie chicken. That's the secret; because it's moist."

Lizzy cringed. She was one of those people who couldn't stand the word "*moist*." Exactly why he chose to use it.

"Grapes are the other secret ingredient—chopped-up, juicy red grapes."

Lizzy looked skeptical but impressed.

He had, in fact, made the chicken salad. Adam spent a lot of time in the kitchen with the family cook, Marge, growing up. He enjoyed helping her and chatting with her. With Marge, Adam could be himself. He didn't have to play any roles or personas. Marge would've liked Katherine. He was sure of it. His mom? He really didn't care what she thought. She would assume Katherine was just another game—a way to kill time. But she felt different; she was different.

The picnic was fabulous. He had planned it out perfectly. If only he could get Lizzy and Brandon to take off together again.

When they were young, Brandon and Adam had decided they would be perfect wingmen. They developed a discreet signal for when they wanted privacy—a little hand signal. Adam was just about to give the sign when Brandon gave it.

Adam paused, internally questioning if the signal was meant for Brandon and his sister. His sister!

"Lizzy, I heard someone say there are baby bunnies around that way. I know how you love that. Brandon can take some pictures of them for you." Not very subtle, but it did the job. Adam just hoped Katherine didn't want to see them too.

Lizzy was thrilled with the idea of more alone time, but she stopped herself. "Are you guys coming?"

Without any hesitation and exaggerated fake disappointment, Katherine replied, "Not me, thanks. You guys go ahead. Not sure that path would be good for my ankle. I can't wait to see the pictures."

"I'm going to stay back with Katie," Adam chimed in.

Brandon sighed, frustrated the damn pictures were brought up again! He made a mental note never to mention photography again. If Katherine stuck around, he'd need to fake carpal tunnel or vision changes. He wasn't about to complain—more time alone with Lizzy. He wondered if Adam thought the hand signal he gave was so he and Katherine could have time together. If so, that was good. He wasn't ready for that conversation. How did one tell their best friend he'd been in love with his little sister since middle school?

Lizzy was thrilled Adam was spending time alone with Katherine, and she was getting more time with Brandon. If she could get Adam into a real relationship, Lizzy thought she might have a chance with Brandon. There was nothing they didn't know about each other. Through Adam, they had heard all about each other's games. Aside from Adam, Brandon was the only person who knew the real her. They were always becoming what people wanted or expected, especially with their parents. Their mom's motto was to "Read the room and become who you need to be."

Growing up, Lizzy and Adam were taught the game. They would pretend to be different people in different situations. If their dad had a client over who loved theater, they all loved theater. If the client loved the outdoors, they loved the outdoors. Art lovers? What a coincidence; they were studying art history. They played the game so often they would sometimes get confused.

Lizzy had once bought Adam new skis; he had never skied. Then there was the time he bought her tickets to the opening of some modern dance group. He was so excited to have gotten such a thoughtful gift and was sure she'd love it. The blank look on her face said it all.   "You don't like modern dance, do you?"

Unlike Adam, Brandon never got confused. He paid attention and saw her—the real her.

***

Chris stopped dead in her tracks. That laugh sounded just like Lizzy's. She could see them through the bushes. They looked like two couples out for a romantic hike. She felt a warm fondness for the group, followed by a building white-hot rage. The four of them went, leaving her out!

Her thoughts hijacked her mood. *What's so damn funny? Why wasn't I invited?*

After all, she was the hiker in the group, for heaven's sake. She even worked as a trail guide during the tourist season.

Unable to shake the sight of the four of them, Chris cut her hike short. No one had ever shown an interest in hiking with her. What else had she missed? How long had this been going on?

She went straight home, undressed, and climbed into bed. She pouted and whined to her dog. "That's another thing. Everyone is so excited about Katherine's dog. I've had a dog for years, and no one cares!"

Shadow looked up at Chris with a big, sloppy grin.

She had to smile. "Yes, baby, I know you love me. I love you too. But it still hurts."

Opening her bedside table, she pulled out a prescription bottle. *Just one. Just one.* The single sleeping pill was so tiny it required no water. Taking it, Chris laid back. Staring at the ceiling, her mind raced until she fell asleep. Shadow curled up next to her.

Chapter II

The hike was great. I made good progress with Adam and successfully paired up Lizzy and Brandon. Adam wasn't my concern the next morning; Chris was. I saw her watching us. I should have gotten her aside sooner. Hopefully, I hadn't dropped the ball.

Chris was tricky. She had so many layers of phony personas. I wasn't sure where her true self began. I needed to make sure I didn't touch on the wrong one.

I pulled out my notebook and tried to figure out what I knew about her. She went to boarding school—true. She said it was a great experience—false. She enjoyed hiking—true. I could tell by her gear she was an avid, experienced hiker. But connecting on that would tip off that I saw her. Shopping? No, I could tell she did that for Lizzy's benefit. She didn't enjoy it. I needed to do some research.

The more I dug, the sadder I found Chris's story. Class photos from several boarding schools showed a different Chris in each picture. She had been trying to fit in for so long, I wasn't sure she knew who she was. After hours of pouring through social media posts, blogs, and news articles, I saw it. A report from fifteen years ago about a boarding school's new art program, thanks to a wealthy benefactor. I saw her—seven or eight years old, happily painting with a talented hand and eye. I was sure she still had the talent and passion.

Turning my research to painting, art classes, and art exhibits, I found it—an article about an art outreach program every Sunday afternoon in the park, complete with a photo. Chris was pictured as the teacher and organizer. Gotcha.

The next Sunday, Ruby and I headed to the park. I circled around to get a good look before being seen. Chris looked utterly different and in her element. Her hair was pulled back in an imperfect sloppy bun. She was wearing old, ripped jeans, not trendy ripped but truly worn-out old jeans with old paint smudges—as if she mindlessly wiped paint off her hands on to her legs and butt over time. Her men's flannel shirt was also worn and ripped with the same smudges.

She was a natural with the kids, and she looked undeniably happy. I could hear her laugh—so different from the practiced, controlled laugh I'd heard before. Her posture was relaxed, and she looked comfortable in her own skin.

Such a different Chris outside the group.

I was almost afraid to interrupt. I hated the idea of ruining this escape for her, but maybe I could help her become more confident outside this environment.

When I was ready, Chris saw me. She looked like she didn't know if she should hide or wave. Not giving her a choice, I waved and ran over with Ruby.

"Oh my Gawd! Chris? Is that you? It is you! What are you doing here?"

Chris returned in kind, "Katie! Hi!"

I immediately saw her posture change and her mind start to race. I needed to put her at ease.

"Look at you! You look incredible."

Chris genuinely looked confused by my statement.

Quick, I thought, *change the subject. Get her mind off how she's not in character.*

"I didn't know you painted, and these kids just adore you!"

I saw her soften at the mention of the kids. I decided to stay there. I asked her a bunch of questions about the kids and the program. I could see Chris had a love for what she was doing there. It seemed like she forgot all about Lizzy and the group.

I joined the class, interacting with the kids and painting. It was a lot of fun, and Ruby loved the extra attention from the kids.

After class, Chris and I took a walk around the lake. I was surprised by how much she was willing to share. Seemed like a dam had opened, and once it started, she couldn't help herself. I got the backstory and dirt on everyone, even some little tidbits I didn't know. It seemed like Chris had been a sponge, sitting back and watching quietly for a long time.

Need to be careful not to pry too much.

Chris was like a stray kitten who scared easily. I didn't want her to rethink what she was revealing. Rule of thumb: When someone was gossiping, let them talk. Just nod and gently guide the conversation along with short building questions. Don't give them the chance to rethink what they're sharing.

Ruby and I were both exhausted and dropped on the couch as soon as we got home. I wasn't sure what to do with all the information I learned. I had a growig suspicion that while I was playing them, they were playing me. Excited about the new twist, I opened my journal and started writing.

***

Chris couldn't believe Katie was in the park earlier that day. She felt a real connection with her and couldn't remember when she ever felt so at ease and accepted. Sitting in her apartment, she started to question the entire encounter.

Is it too good to be true? Did I talk too much? I probably bored her to death, and she's having a good laugh at my expense with Lizzy right now.

Becoming overwhelmed with anxiety, Chris picked up the phone to call Lizzy and quickly put it back down. *Wait. Slow down. I need a reason to call.*

She picked up the phone again, deciding instead to just make something up. The sad reality was that Lizzy didn't really listen to Chris, and Chris knew it.

"Hi, Lizzy…"

There was no need for her to come up with a story or reason for the call because it seemed Lizzy couldn't wait to tell her all about Brandon and the hike. After an hour of listening, Chris hung up the phone, relieved Katherine hadn't said anything. If she had, Lizzy definitely would have mentioned it.

The next day, Chris sat opposite her therapist, who was seated upright yet relaxed in chair that matched the design of her own, only smaller. The big, oversized chair made her feel like a little girl sitting across the room from a motherly figure in her perfectly sized chair. She wondered if the design was intentional and if all her patients sat in these chairs or only the ones in need of a caring mother figure.

Her therapist was the leader in the field of self-identity. When she first learned about Dr. Laurie Stewart, she was only a teenager. Her art teacher had recommended Chris read the doctor's coming-of-age book on finding oneself. It resonated so much that she sought out and devoured all her books. When she moved to be near Lizzy after graduation, she learned the doctor saw patients an hour away. She had been seeing her once a week since to work on confidence and self-concept.

Chris was doing her best to replay everything that happened with Katherine. She knew the doctor would see it as a breakthrough. She lowered her walls and let someone in, even if it wasn't intentional. Chris felt really proud of herself and needed approval.

Usually, her doctor wouldn't voice her opinions. Instead, she would gently encourage Chris to come to her own conclusions. However, Dr. Stewart knew this was just what Chris needed. Those other so-called friends were a bad influence on her. The doctor encouraged Chris not to overthink it and recommended she pursue this friendship.

Chris glanced at the clock on the wall and wondered if she had enough time to tell the doctor about being left out of the hiking trip. She was curious about what her thoughts were on it. That's when the framed photo on the desk caught her eye. Getting up from her comfortable chair, she walked over and picked it up. "I'm sorry, but who is that?"

"That's my daughter."

"She looks so familiar," Chris said, studying the photo closer. "Actually, she looks a lot like Katherine."

Dr. Stewart explained how after speaking about Katherine the entire session, she was on Chris's mind. "I bet you can see Katherine in me as well."

Chris looked closely at the doctor and laughed. "You're right! That's so interesting."

Once Chris left the office, the doctor called her daughter and left a message on her voicemail. "It's your mother. You're working one of my clients. Call me."

***

My mom could be so dramatic. How was I supposed to know Chris was one of her patients? Rather than thank me, which she should have, she demanded I watch my step, as if she didn't teach me everything she knew. Due to patient confidentiality, she would never say anything more, but it was rather obvious.

"Listen, Mom, the student surpassed the master years ago. I know how to cover my tracks. Why the hell do you have a picture of me on your desk? That's your mistake, not mine."

"I'm a proud mom. I can't tell anyone what you do. The least you can let me do is have a photo on my desk."

I rolled my eyes at the phone, and Ruby barked in the background.

"Don't tell me you got a dog!"

"I'll talk to you later, Mom."

"Have I taught you nothing?"

I hung up.

Turning to Ruby, I said, "That's it. You blew it. Now my mom knows. Don't wag your tail at me. She'll be buying you those dumb dog sweaters before you know it. She always wanted to be a grandma."

Chapter 12

"Adam! Hi!" I placed an actual call, not a text. "I was just thinking about you." I really was, but not the way he hoped.

"Katherine, I was just about to call you! Dinner—just the two of us." It sounded less like a question and more of a command.

"That sounds wonderful. What did you have in mind?"

"Dinner at The Tree—tomorrow at nine p.m. I'll pick you up at eight thirty." Again, not a question.

Fabulous—a fancy, overpriced, obnoxious restaurant to try to win me over.

I took a deep breath and did my best to sound thrilled. "Great! Wait, don't you need my address?"

"Oh…um…yeah. What's your address?"

I gave Adam the address he already had. "Can't miss it, It's the light-blue Victorian with the stone front porch."

A quick Google search confirmed The Tree was a trendy new restaurant. It looked like Adam was pulling some strings. Reservations were full weeks in advance. Thankfully, everyone who had been able to eat there felt compelled to post photos of their experience on social media, so I knew what to expect as I scanned over dozens of pictures of food that looked pretty and was hopefully tasty.

I came across photos of the grand opening.

Lookie here. Is Adam an owner? How did I miss this? Nowhere in any of the articles was his name listed. But there he was in all the photos. *That's odd—a search of the business doesn't name him as an owner.*

Looking over all the pictures again, I didn't see anyone else from the group.

Back in my beach home, I packed a bag with an assortment of things I might need. I was staying at the Victorian house now, returning only for supplies. Now that my address was known, I'd need to stay there regularly.

I looked for an appropriate date outfit. This project was taking my wardrobe to its limits. A lot of girls assumed sexy meant revealing, tight, trashy little outfits. Not true. Sexy was anything that made someone feel confident. Something that showed a person's shape without revealing it. Something that made a man imagine what was underneath. An outfit they could imagine taking off.

For dinner, I chose a long, modest sundress that was open in the back and held up with a single tie. It was a soft, touchable material. A pretty, solid coral color paired with my nude strappy sandals. Sandals could be a turnoff. Some people hated feet, while others obsessed over them. Thanks to my weekly pedicure, I was safe either way.

After unpacking, I walked around the house, strategically placing my own photos and items. I'd miss this house and its neighbors. The old man next door walked over every time he saw me and offered me peppers from his garden. The mom across the street had begun saving me a cupcake or slice of banana bread when she baked. It was nice.

I could never live someplace like this. Neighbors would quickly become suspicious of different characters walking out the door. The thought of it was actually pretty funny. They would probably think I had multiple-personality disorder. The real owner, an older woman, traveled for work so often the neighbors had no clue I wasn't her. It couldn't have worked out better.

Naturally, Adam would pick me up for our date tomorrow. It was a quick turnaround. He seemed anxious. Maybe Lizzy and Brandon partnering up had left him a little desperate, lonely, and most likely bored.

Ruby and I sat on the front porch with a glass of wine. I jotted down some more notes in my notebook. I couldn't keep him at arm's length much longer; no one wanted to play a game they weren't winning at. He needed a win. My project didn't have to be all work. I could have some fun too.

Let's see what you got, Adam.

He was prompt, appearing with a single sunflower. I smiled—sunflowers are actually my favorite. A single flower was very thoughtful. Anyone could grab a pre-packaged bouquet of flowers or roses. A single flower showed a deliberate, thoughtful choice.

The look in his eyes said it all: the sundress was the right choice. We were off to a great start. We arrived at the restaurant. Valet parking, of course. They were packed. People were gathered in groups large and small around the outside of the building. Heaters and benches scattered by the front door and along the front of the building helped keep the crowd comfortable. No one looked even remotely annoyed by the wait. Everyone seemed happy to be there.

We walked to the front and were quickly welcomed and ushered to a small private table in the back corner. This place was really charming. It was upscale, yes, but so warm and inviting. Adam stood as he was welcomed by a petite woman in a chef's jacket. She was genuinely happy to see him and gave him a hug.

When she saw me, she smiled and said to him, "¡Finalmente estás con alguien, ella debe ser muy especial!" With a laugh, she addressed both of us. "What can I make you guys? I hope you're hungry."

"Surprise us. We trust that whatever you make will be delicious," Adam replied.

With that, she left to talk to our server.

"I hope you don't mind. I've learned to let the chef serve whatever she feels is the best choice for the night. The menu is designed to direct you toward options which make the most return, not that anything on the menu wouldn't be amazing. She's really an amazing chef."

"Do you know what she said to you, Adam? Do you speak Spanish?" I knew what she said. I was fluent in Spanish, but I was curious to hear his response.

"Yes, I speak Spanish; and a little French, by the way," he said, flashing his charming smile. "She said I am a fortunate man to be out with such a beautiful woman."

I pretended to blush. That was not what she said. She said it was about time he brought someone around. *I'm guessing he doesn't come here with dates.*

Someone brought over an expensive-looking bottle of wine. Without even glancing at it, Adam waved for it to be served. He didn't want to taste it first. He motioned for me to try it.

I took a tentative sip. My eyes opened wide. "This is really good!"

"You sound so surprised, Kate." Adam had started calling me "Kate" recently, as opposed to Lizzy's "Katie." It was an old trick, and I knew it. Nicknames could make a person feel important and close.

"This is really good. What is it?" I genuinely wanted to know. I wanted more. I looked at the label, "Pasovimo Vineyards? I've never heard of it."

He was very pleased with himself and looked like a little kid dying to tell a secret. "It's an unassuming little vineyard up north. A small family business passed down for generations. I happened across it entirely by accident and fell in love with their natural smooth taste, and the family is very kind and sweet." He took a long, self-indulgent sip. "The grandmother—the third generation to operate the vineyard—was a spitfire of a woman. She told it like it was and didn't apologize for it. Very rare in her time. She took control of the business from her father, who was an alcoholic." He paused to make sure he had my attention.

It was a great story, and I wondered if it was true. I didn't care either way. I leaned forward, sipping my glass of wine, encouraging him to continue.

"You see, her father inherited the vineyard already in disrepair. Unable to deal with the mess, he self-medicated. As an alcoholic, he couldn't really taste how bad his own product was. The wine was undrinkable—worse than the worst. This little woman stepped in and took over. Stopped all production. She tossed it all. Cleaned out the neglected barrels. She was only sixteen at the time, mind you. At first, the employees wouldn't listen to a woman, so many of them quit. You can find a few rare bottles from before her father's time, and they're good. But her early years are unparalleled. She passed it on to her daughter, much to the dismay of her son, and her daughter continues to produce above par vintages. The next generation is preparing to take over after achieving a degree and completing her internship in Italy. I predict the next generation will really put this company on the map."

Adam was a fantastic storyteller. He missed his calling as a writer, for sure. He had me hanging on his every word.

"Not sure if I believe the entire story, but the wine is fantastic."

He dramatically faked being insulted. "It's mostly true. I go every fall to sample the most recent vintage and buy a case or two. This bottle is from my personal inventory."

Conversation flowed effortlessly. I had to occasionally remind myself that I was Katherine. The food was remarkable, and I forgave him for ordering for me. Dessert was a phenomenal personal-sized white chiffon cake with fresh fruit and a small dollop of whipped cream on the side. The edges had a slight crisp to them, and the inside was light and fluffy. Every bite melted in my mouth. With perfect timing, the chef returned to give us both big hugs goodbye. I noticed there was no check. We just got up and left.

The next stop was a leisurely stroll on the beach. The sand was so cold and soft underfoot. Truth be told, sometimes I missed having this on my side of the bridge. It was a beautiful clear night with a bright moon and tons of stars in the sky. Before I knew it, the sun was rising. Adam was the perfect gentleman.

Once we got to my house, Adam leaned over and briefly brushed his lips against mine. As he pulled away, I found myself leaning forward, wanting more. He winked at me and commented on how poor Ruby probably needed to pee.

Shit, I forgot all about the dog. I hoped she didn't do anything to the house while I was gone. With that thought firmly planted in my head, I sprang from the car and ran to the house. "Oh, Ruby, I'm so sorry. I'm coming!"

I could hear him laughing as he drove away. A moment later I received a text:

> I had a great time.
>
> I hope Ruby is OK.
>
> Annual group trip this weekend to the family cabin.
>
> I hope you can come.

Thankfully, Ruby and the house were both fine.

The next day, Lizzy followed up with her own invite. I accepted, but with this group, I had no idea what to expect. Deciding I needed more information, I called Chris.

Chris was delighted that I was invited to the cabin and even more so that her opinion was sought.

"Promise you'll room with me! It'll be so much fun. And make sure you pack toilet paper!" Chris burst out laughing.

"Seriously, do I need dressy clothes? Active?"

Focus, Chris. I need real information from you.

"It's really low key. Pack a couple of bathing suits and comfortable clothes. Oh, a rain jacket and boots. I think it might rain."

Chapter 13

An SUV pulled up, and Adam was driving. Chris, Lizzy, Brandon, and Matt were already packed in. Adam jumped out and grabbed my bag off the porch and greeted me with a kiss on the cheek. "Sorry, Brandon already called shotgun." He looked heartbroken about it.

Brandon shrugged. "Rules are rules."

I stopped Matt from climbing into the back. "I'm smaller. I'll take the third row." Matt looked around for permission, afraid he was going to get into trouble.

"I insist. End of discussion." I climbed in next to Chris.

With a shrug, Matt returned to his seat next to Lizzy.

"Everyone settled?" Adam called out from the driver's seat. "Last call."

The three-hour drive flew by, with blasting music and road-trip snacks being passed around. We only stopped once—a very cliché, small gas station, rest stop, grocery store, bait shop type of place. It reminded me of a 1980s horror movie. The kind the group of teens stopped at. A small, rundown, side-of-the road store where an old man or woman warned them to turn back.

"This is the last of civilization before the cabin. They sell just about everything you can imagine. We always stop here for last-minute snacks, milk, etcetera," Chris explained to me as everyone stiffly exited the car.

"I don't know why you have to act like a sitcom dad on these trips. Would it kill you to stop once or twice?" Lizzy stretched her legs. With a smirk, she said, "And by the way, shotgun home."

"No, it's too early to call it. That's cheating," Adam replied.

Brandon whispered something in Lizzy's ear, and she laughed. "You're right. Never mind. I'll take a turn in the third row." With a wink at Brandon, she ran into the store.

Adam helped me out of the car. "It's only another thirty minutes or so. How are you doing back there?"

Standing upright and stretching my arms above my head, I said, "I have to agree with Lizzy. At least one stop before now would have been nice."

Overhearing me, Brandon shouted, "Save your breath. It'll never happen. Be thankful he agrees to stop here."

"It's a family tradition," Adam said quietly. "Sorry. You good?"

"Yeah, I'm fine. The third row is roomier than you'd think."

"Come on. They have the best homemade cookies here." Taking my hand, we joined the others to grab last-minute supplies.

Chris had said the cabin was ordinary, but I never in a million years would have expected such a charming lakeside cottage: a huge front porch, two floors, a modest three bedrooms, one-and-a-half baths, and an outhouse—an honest-to-God wooden outhouse.

But that wasn't the most surprising part.

The cabin had a warm, inviting feel to it. The rooms were cluttered with old family photos on the walls and random keepsakes on the shelves.

We dropped our bags at the door. Adam walked around, hitting switches and waking up the sleeping cabin. Everyone talked at once while unpacking groceries. It seemed like they had a routine. I took the opportunity to wander around and look at the photos.

One photo in particular caught my eye—a big old frame with dozens of small images in a makeshift collage. They looked like candid snapshots from someone's college years. But one person in several pictures looked just like my mother.

Laughing, Lizzy came over. "My mom made that her senior year of college. Said it was the best four years of her life. That's her there."

"They look like a tight group. Are they still close?"

"Not that I know of. I think they had a falling out about something." Lizzy shrugged. "This is the photo you want to see." Walking further down the hall, she directed my attention to a photo in a small, tacky, gold-plated frame. There, in all his naked glory, was a five-year-old Adam jumping off the dock into the lake.

"Lizzy! If you're showing her that lake photo, I swear I'm going to pull out the album from your middle school years!" Adam yelled down the hallway.

"Don't you dare. I should have burned that book when I had the chance!" she yelled back, running out into the living room.

While Lizzy and Adam were occupied with their playful sibling fight, which sounded like it had gotten physical, Chris grabbed my arm and pulled me into a small downstairs room. It was super tiny, but the dark paneling made it seem even more so. It barely fit the one dresser and bunk beds. "Since it's your first visit, I'll let you choose: upper or lower?"

Adam suddenly filled the doorway. "Whatcha doin' in here?"

Chris was quick to reply. "Just helping Katherine get settled."

"In here?" He looked confused.

I laughed. "Where did you think I would sleep, Adam?"

Chris and I waited for a response.

"I, um, I assumed you'd stay with Lizzy."

"Guess again." Brandon popped up behind Adam and, with a playful punch to the arm, ran off.

Adam looked pale and yelled after him, "Wait, what?"

That pairing up worked perfectly. With Lizzy and Brandon in one room together, the remaining four would naturally split boys and girls. No way Chris and Matt were sharing a room, even if it was the bunk beds.

Adam grilled burgers, and we all sat around playing old board games. It was so quiet and relaxing, Lizzy dozed off on Brandon's shoulder. She startled herself awake with her own dainty snore.

"I think that's our cue." With a general goodnight wave to the group, Brandon and Lizzy headed off to bed.

"I guess that's a wrap. Good night." Matt jumped up, looking relieved for the opportunity to exit.

"I'm going to stay up and do the dishes." Adam glanced at me.

Rather than reply with the, "I'll help," he wanted, I said, "Great, I'll do tomorrows."

We left Adam alone to clean up.

Chris was exhausted and fell right to sleep, leaving me to wonder if staying up with Adam would have been more productive. I wish I could have brought my journal. I took some time to type random reminders on my phone before going to sleep.

At dawn, I spotted Matt sitting on the dock from the kitchen window. Taking an extra mug of coffee with me, I walked down. I hated that Jennifer left him broken. That wasn't my intent.

I handed him a mug and sat.

We sat side by side, staring out at the water, swinging our feet, and drinking coffee in silence for a while.

"I know you're not her," Matt said, breaking the silence but not his stare at the horizon. Matt seemed relaxed. "I really do."

"I would tell you it's better to have loved and lost than to have never loved yada, yada." I turned to Matt. "But that's a load of crap. Love hurts. Plain and simple."

Matt continued to stare forward. "You're not helping."

"I know. Sorry." After a moment of silence, I continued. "The way I see it, it's what you learn from the relationship that matters." I paused and decided to give a little push. "Pretend I'm her. Pretend I'm Jennifer. What do you want to say?"

Matt turned to me and looked deep into my eyes.

Am I really this good? He really doesn't see Jennifer.

Finally, with a deep, long sigh, he said, "I guess I would say thank you."

"Thank you?" I didn't see that coming.

Turning his attention to the horizon, he continued. "It's like you said. It's what you learn. I never really thought of it that way. But Jennifer taught me a lot about myself. She showed me who I can be outside this group."

So, this isn't about Jennifer. It's about the group.

"Can I tell you a secret?" he asked, shifting his attention back to me.

I nodded.

He returned his eyes back to the lake. "They all assume I was heartbroken and in some sort of depression, and I was, but not for long. Adam came over and got me up and out of the house. And I'm grateful for that. But since then, I've been trying to get away from them." He paused, looking in my eyes to make sure he had my attention. "Don't get drawn in. They'll suck your life from you." Matt got up and walked up to the house, finding Adam on the deck looking out.

***

"Hey, what's up with that?" Adam asked Matt, nodding toward the deck.

"Nothing, we were just talking."

"About me?"

"Yea, she was telling me she thinks you're an ass." Matt laughed. "Relax, we were talking about the weather. Everyone up?"

"Yea, Chris is in the shower, Brandon and Lizzy are um, awake."

"Shit, how you doing? Your sister and best friend?" He shook his head sympathetically.

"Yea, makes me feel bad about that time with your sister."

Matt hit Adam, "You really are an ass. I'm so glad you never met my sister. I'm gonna change. Go talk to her, before everyone comes out."

***

Adam snuck up behind me and pretended to push me in.

My heart was racing, I wasn't expecting that.

He sat behind me, straddled me, and kissed my neck. "Good Morning."

"Brandon, is that you?"

"Not funny, Lizzy would kill you."

I laughed and leaned back on Adam, sipping my coffee. "Matt was just telling me it's going to be hot today. Any chance on seeing that naked tush jump off the dock again?"

"Maybe we can sneak out tomorrow morning for a skinny dip," Adam wiggled his eyebrows.

"Maybe."

"Why not now?" Brandon suddenly appeared, and with a big shove, launched both of us into the water.

"Brandon! Oh Shit! It's cold!" Adam was a bit of a wuss about it.

Brandon was hysterically laughing as he hit the water moments after us courtesy of Matt, who, being the only dressed in a swimsuit, joined us in the water with a huge cannonball.

"Come on, join us! It's cold but great!" Adam called out to Lizzy and Chris, who were watching at a safe distance.

"Hell no, it's too early." Lizzy shouted back.

"Hold on, I'll get towels." Chris ran into the house. She liked to be helpful.

I left the boys horse playing in the water and went to change out of my wet clothes and into a bathing suit.

It was a hot day, but a breeze off the water made it ideal for a full day of water skiing, swimming, and sunning.

The cabin was stocked with prepared meals. Chris put the side dishes in the oven and set the table as Matt put steaks on the BBQ.

Brandon made a campfire out by the water. As the sun set and the temperature dropped, it was a perfect way to end the day.

The rest of the weekend was rainy. Confining everyone to the cabin. Adam kept trying unsuccessfully to get me alone, but the cabin was so small there really wasn't any place to be alone, not even the bathroom. You couldn't be in there for more than a couple of minutes without someone banging on the door. No one wanted to run to the outhouse in the rain, although it was cute and charming. It even had a little moon-shaped window cut out of the door.

The time passed playing games, doing puzzles, watching old movies, singing and dancing.

The drive home was uneventful, Lizzy and Brandon slept in the third row, Chris and I sat in the middle, and Matt won shotgun in an impromptu card game.

After the confession, Matt seemed to relax and loosen up. I didn't think any of us would see him again after that weekend. It felt like he was saying his goodbyes to this chapter of his life.

It seemed like both Matt and Chris would be better off without this group.

I guess they aren't as tight as I thought.

This was quickly turning into my favorite project.

Chapter 14

As soon as I got home, I called my mom. She picked up on the first ring, assuming something was wrong. She never heard from me during a project.

"Is everything OK?"

"Yeah, Mom, so listen, you're not going to believe this. I think you know their mom."

"Whose mom? I'm so confused. You never tell me about your project while you're working."

"Ugh, let's just say I was at someone's family cabin, and there was a photo on the wall, *and you were in it!*"

"That seems unlikely, honey. Are you sure?"

"Yes, Mom, I am! They were all taken at a college in Boston. You were in a dozen or so photos in a collage with a girl with short blond hair. In some pictures, her hair looked blue."

"Holy shit! Oh my God."

"Mom, why are you shouting?"

"I can't believe it. It can't be. It just can't!"

"Mom, you're scaring me."

"I'm sorry. What's the family's last name? You have to give me that."

"I really don't think I should. Not now, anyway. Just tell me: Is there something I should know? I really like this project. I'd hate to bail early."

"Remember the story I told you about my college roommate?"

I knew immediately what she was talking about. That story was a vital part of who she was today.

"No way! Well, that makes this all really interesting."

***

Katherine's mom, Laurie, met Lizzy and Adam's mom, Barbara, during her freshman year of college. They were randomly assigned to be roommates and were quickly inseparable. Although they had different classes, they lived and worked together on campus.

One afternoon, while walking to the library, they passed an unusually packed convention hall. That was when Laurie had an idea. She grabbed Barbara's arm and said, "I need to pee. Come with me."

Together they walked into the convention center. Laurie took a quick assessment of the crowd and posters hanging around as they made their way to a restroom.

"Here's the deal: This is a national company retreat. There are so many people here. There's no way they all know each other." Taking a quick look in the mirror, Laurie fixed her hair. "Clean yourself up a little. We're gonna have some fun and a good meal. We might even get some parting gifts!"

"Laurie, I can't get kicked out of school. It's my only chance." Barbara was a goody two shoes and not a risk taker. But she was a follower who gravitated to anyone who took the lead. Since coming to school, that lead had been Laurie.

"What are they going to do? Ask us to leave? So we get caught, we go to the library, and make ramen later. We're not breaking any laws. Besides, who's gonna question us?"

Taking a good look at herself in the mirror, Barbara pulled out her messy ponytail, using a little water to flatten it out, then she followed Laurie out the door.

Laurie picked up two folders from a table and handed one to Barbara. "This is how we look like we belong."

"Laurie, this is stealing!"

"Barb, it's a folder with paper in it. It's not for sale. It doesn't belong to anyone. It's not stealing."

Barbara opened hers and looked inside. It was just photocopies of schedules and brochures.

Minutes later someone approached them, introducing themselves.

Laurie was quick to respond. "Hi, I'm Bridgette, from the Midwest, and this is Peggy."

Barbara could feel and hear her heart beating out of her chest. Taking a breath, she extended her hand. "Nice to meet you."

Laurie turned the conversation outward and kept people talking about themselves. Whenever anyone asked them about their role in the company, Laurie replied with different renditions of the same stock answer: "Oh, aren't you tired of talking about work? I'd much rather learn about you. Are you married? Kids?"

Barbara was in awe of how natural Laurie was and let her do most of the talking. They spent the entire day as Bridgette and Peggy, talking to people, drinking, and eating. As predicted, they even got little bags full of products.

It was so much fun to be someone else. Barbara and Laurie were hooked, getting better and more daring as time went on. Crashing weddings, conventions, and getting into events became a hobby.

While Laurie was having fun meeting and learning about people by assimilating into different groups. Barbara was learning to manipulate individuals.

Senior year, Barbara started going out on her own with different men. Laurie was concerned. These weren't college guys, they were older men, some married, the occasional professor.

"Barbara, what are you doing? Where did the TV come from? And the jewelry?"

"I can't help it if people want to give me gifts."

"Why, why are they giving you gifts? Who?"

"Don't take that tone with me. You're jealous. You do your research and I do mine."

Laurie never brought it up again.

The different philosophies would be what eventually destroyed their friendship.

Laurie was a natural at fitting into different groups by getting people to talk about themselves, later becoming a remarkably successful and famous therapist and self-help author.

Barbara had to work at it, but she enjoyed the power it gave her, becoming skilled at manipulating people. Using what she learned from Laurie, Barbara went on to snag a gorgeous, rich husband and was able to make him more powerful and wealthy with the help of her children.

***

Well, this was an interesting turn of events. What exactly was his objective? Was I being played just for the fun of it? That would probably explain the Tiff scene. She was a fun game that he got bored of. Did I need to change Katherine at all with this new development? No, Katherine moved into the group seamlessly. Adam was trying hard to play me. I knew it, but now that I knew who his mother was, things just got more interesting. This was definitely my favorite project.

I pulled out my daily planner. I needed to wrap up this project before the house-sitting gig was up. With all these plot twists and turns, I wasn't sure which path to take. Monday mornings I ran with Lizzy. Lizzy and

Brandon were now attached at the hip. He was teaching her to surf, so she had less time and energy to run. No complaints from me.

Then there was Chris. I liked her. With Lizzy preoccupied with Brandon, this was her chance to make a clean break. She was definitely better off without this group and would need support, and a few gentle nudges. I decided to make spending Sunday mornings in the park with Chris a regular thing. Chris never mentioned it to Lizzy. I was confident I would have heard about it if she had. Matt was now a nonissue, not coming around anymore. It was time to focus on my main character: Adam.

****

I fell asleep on the couch. A frantic knock at the door scared the crap out of me. Maybe someone's house was on fire. What if this house was on fire? Dressed in a tank top, pajama pants, and a really messy bun, I ran to open the door.

The last thing I expected to find was a soaking wet Adam on the other side.

No words were necessary. I opened the door and stepped aside to let him in. This was an Adam I had never seen before.

I closed the door and turned around to find he had not moved. He just stood there.

"Adam?"

"I didn't know where else to go. I didn't have anywhere else I wanted to go." Adam looked me in the eyes and hugged me. I felt his entire body relax, and he slowly began to sob.

What the actual fuck is going on?

My heart broke a little for him. Whatever was going on, it was not good, and it was not an act. He was not that good. I wasn't even that good.

I took his face in my hands, pushed him back, and looked him in the eyes. "Are you OK?"

As his sobbing came to an end, I took him to the bathroom. "Let's get you out of these wet clothes. There is a robe on the door and towels in the closet. Would you like a drink?"

With a deep sigh, he turned his back to me and started to undress. "Hot coffee would be nice. I'm freezing."

I backed out of the room before any more clothing could come off. *Damn, he looks good enough to eat.*

He emerged from the bathroom much calmer and dressed in my fuzzy teal robe. Handing him a mug of coffee, I walked to the couch and sat down silently. I waited. He followed, pulling a blanket over his legs as he sat. Ruby went over and kissed his face a few times before making herself comfortable on Adam's lap.

"I'm sorry to barge in like this. I can't imagine what you must think."

"I think you need a friend. I'm here if you want to talk."

He cringed a little at the word *friend*, but he knew I was right. He needed a friend right now.

"Growing up, there was only one person I was close to—one person I could be myself with." He sighed. "Before you even say it, no, it's not Lizzy. Definitely not Lizzy." He shook his head at the thought. "Actually, do you have something stronger than coffee? Something I can spike it with?"

I got up and looked through the cabinet by the wine glasses. "How about some Kahlúa?"

"Perfect."

I brought the bottle over and watched as he spiked his coffee with a heavy pour.

"Thanks. Yeah, so definitely not Lizzy. It was Gladys, the family's cook and nanny. She was like a mother to me. She taught me how to cook, do laundry, treat people with respect, and how to love. When she died ten years ago from cancer, it was the hardest thing I had ever faced. My family made crude jokes about needing to break in a new cook and maid. I didn't know she was sick. How did I not know she was dying?"

I could see he was trying to hold back tears.

"At her funeral, I found out she had a family of her own. She was a single mom. She had a daughter and a son. I was relieved and comforted to have people to mourn with. She raised me, too, you know? They felt like family."

"Her children comforted *you*?" I tried to follow the logic.

"Yes, like I said, she was like a mother to me. I was the only one in my family to attend the funeral. Could you imagine?" Adam began to sob again.

I moved to put an arm around him, and he pushed me away, wiping the tears from his face.

Angry, he jumped up and started pacing. Ruby, startled by him, took off for the bedroom. "They said it wouldn't be appropriate. How could it not be appropriate? When someone you love and respect dies, you mourn them. You go to their funeral. You don't just move on!"

He sat back down and looked at me. "I hate them. I just really hate them—even Lizzy. Oh my God, she can be such a heartless bitch."

I wasn't sure what Katherine would say; I didn't know what I would say. I was speechless.

Something must have happened to bring all this up. Gladys had been gone for ten years. "What happened, Adam?"

Adam's shoulders dropped, and he plopped back down on the couch with a heavy sigh. "Gabby, her daughter, was diagnosed with cancer. She called to tell me. Lizzy was there when I took the call. I made the mistake of telling her." He shook his head in disbelief. "I was caught off guard and upset. She asked what was wrong, and I told her." He paused and let out a huff.

"Why was it a mistake?"

"Lizzy had no idea Gladys even had kids. She asked why the hell she would call and tell me. They probably just want money. She had the nerve to ask, 'Didn't we pay that woman enough?' Accused her of stealing our old clothes and leftovers. In Lizzy's mind, we clothed and fed her kids! When I explained how I've kept in touch with them over the years, she accused me of being stupid and played. That was it. I snapped. I called her a heartless, cold, ruthless, self-involved, narcissistic bitch."

"You what?" It took all my self-control not to laugh.

"Something along those lines."

"What did she say?"

"I don't know. I stormed out into the rain until I found myself at your door."

"You walked here?"

Adam reached for the Kahlúa bottle to add more to his cup. I took it from him. "Give me that. I'll get you some more coffee."

"If Lizzy only knew, Kate. If she only knew."

After a long pause, I wasn't sure if he was going to continue. I needed him to keep talking. I returned with a fresh cup of coffee. "Knew what, Adam?"

Adam started laughing. "You know that restaurant I took you to, The Tree? I bought it for them. She cooks, and her brother runs the front. I am so proud of them." His face lit up like a proud parent. "I don't make anything on it. I insisted on being a silent partner they buy out once the restaurant was up and running." He let out another laugh and a smile. "They already bought me out. Gladys did a great job raising them. She would be so proud. That restaurant is one hundred percent their hard work, talent, and dedication. I just wrote the checks."

"That's amazing, Adam, it really is." I meant it. It was incredible that they owned and ran the most successful upscale restaurant on the shore, but it was really amazing that Adam selflessly helped them out of the goodness of his heart and his love for their mom.

"Is she going to be OK? The daughter?"

"Yeah, thankfully. She didn't tell me until she was done with treatment and in remission. That is part of the reason why I'm so upset. They went through this alone; they didn't need or want my support. I'm glad she's OK! Oh God, I'm so glad she's OK. But I thought we were closer than that, and we're not. I wish I could have been there for them, but in the end, I'm just their mom's old boss writing checks."

He leaned over, taking my face in his hands, and looking me in the eyes. "I can't be alone anymore. I need something real. I need someone real." With that, he gently kissed my lips, then laid his head down on my lap and cried himself to sleep.

Chapter 15

The next morning, I woke up on the couch with a throw blanket and Ruby on top of me. No Adam to be found. Only a Post-it note that read:

Pick you up at 11.
Dress comfortable.

In my experience, there was a fine line between a man taking control and a man taking control. The first was sexy and self-confident—an "I'll take care of it for you, My Queen," gesture. The second was arrogant—

"Your opinion does not matter." Adam was walking that line like a tightrope. Eventually, he would reveal which side he fell on. A charming smile and sparkling eyes only took someone so far.

"What do you think, Ruby?" I laughed. "No opinion? Let's go find something comfortable to wear and get ready." I was getting too used to talking to this dog. I wasn't sure if that was a good or bad thing.

At precisely eleven, there was a knock on the door. It was not Adam. It was a driver. He was trying to impress me by throwing around some money. *Fine. Spend away, baby. Spend away.*

The driver told me to bring Ruby along. She seemed happy to not be left home alone.

I climbed into the back of a roomy black car. There was another note:

> It's a long drive. Get comfortable.
> Feel free to nap.

What else was I doing? But Adam didn't know that.

Has your mother taught you nothing, Adam?

For all he knew, I could have had a full day planned. Ruby and I got comfortable with the soft plush throw blanket. She slept while I watched out the window as city turned to highway then farmland.

What do you have planned, Adam? Where the hell are we going?

Surrounded by miles of tan-colored stalks, I could see the destination in the distance. A vast, awe-inspiring, bright colored hot-air balloon. I had never seen one in person, never mind being on one. It was larger and louder than I imagined. I was speechless as we pulled up. Adam was standing there waiting for me—champagne in hand and grinning like a Cheshire cat. Inside the balloon's basket was a tall and skinny operator in a polo, complete with the balloon company logo stitched on the breast. In a matching polo was a short and stocky man standing outside with a little portable step stool. They reminded me of Abbot and Costello.

"I don't know what to say." I really didn't.

Adam handed me a glass of champagne and lifted me into the basket. It was hard to hear over the hot air being propelled into the balloon. He motioned toward the driver, who was cradling Ruby in his arms. The driver gave me a thumbs-up, and Ruby licked his face. I guessed they were going to be fine together.

Costello helped me into the basket and surprised me with his dexterity, effortlessly jumping in after me. Adam smiled and gave a thumbs-up, and up we went. I braced myself for a jolt, but the basket lifted off very slowly and gently. We floated up like a dream. Once we got going, Abbot did not need to fuel the balloon as much, and it became easier to hear. It was peacefully quiet.

We saw nothing but blue skies and farming fields for miles.

"I don't know what to say. This is amazing!"

"You're amazing. I can't thank you enough for last night. That's two nights we spent together." There was that obnoxious but slightly sexy wink again.

The operators started fussing, and I began to worry. "What's going on? Everything OK?"

"We're in position and at one hundred fifty feet. It's time!" Costello exclaimed with a big smile, handing me a harness.

I looked around, confused and concerned. "Time for what?"

"Time to jump." Still trying to hand me a harness, he tried to hide his amusement.

"Adam? What?"

"We're gonna bungee jump!"

"From the balloon? Now?"

"Yes, and yes. Do you trust me?"

Do I trust you? What is this? A movie? No, I don't trust you. What the hell?

Looking around at the workers, I decided I trusted them. "OK, yes, let's do it."

They strapped us in together. I started to feel like I was on one of those stupid TV shows about extreme dates. Actually, I may have seen this date. *Oh, you sly SOB. You saw this date on TV.*

The idea of jumping off an unstable object with a bungee cord attached to my ankles made me wish the champagne was something stronger.

"On three. One… Two…" Abbot gave us a push.

They do that so you can't back out or try to grab hold of something. I should have seen that coming. The pressure inside my body could only be relieved by a scream. Adam was way ahead of me on that front, screaming in my ear. It was the first pull back on the bungee cord that scared the crap out of me. After that, it was all just fun.

I couldn't stop laughing. Adam kissed me hard and forceful. There was that delicate line again. This time he was definitely on the side of sexy. We stayed in an embrace, laughing and breathless as they pulled us up. Soon after, the balloon landed in a clearing and left us. We appeared to be alone. All I could hear were birds chirping and the sound of running water.

"This is part of a little-known bird sanctuary. There's an outhouse just down that path." Adam pointed down a hiking trail with neon pink stakes marking the way.

"And this way…" He took my hand and lead me down to a stream where lunch was laid out and waiting for us. I was surprised by how hungry I felt and realized I hadn't eaten all day.

I looked over at Adam. He had a sappy puppy dog "Ain't I wonderful?" look on his face.

Oh, this is where I fall all over you? In what? Appreciation? Not so fast, buddy.

I looked around and didn't see much of anything or anyone around. Someone had to set this up. The drinks were cold, and the food was hot. I had no idea exactly where we were, but I was not scared of him. I was a third-degree black belt and had knocked out bigger guys without breaking a sweat. I sat on the cheesy red-and-white-checkered blanket and waited for him to open the wine and serve me.

Wanna be the big man in charge? I can sit back and play a damsel in distress.

Lunch was a delicious grilled chicken panini with just enough melted cheese and roasted veggies. As we ate, Adam proceeded to share his life story—a lot of stuff I already knew from research the night before—leaving out all the details about the game he and his family played. A couple of new details about Lizzy and Brandon: The three of them were inseparable growing up. He was comfortable with Lizzy and Brandon dating and felt like he could trust Brandon. He was happy for them but enjoyed giving them a hard time.

Adam's family, being new money, invested in the club Brandon's family owned when it hit a bad spot years ago. The partnership was exactly what Adam's mom needed to solidify her position in society. Brandon's family was from old money and the name was well respected. Seemed Brandon's family ran through money fast with bad and sloppy investments. When Brandon refused to work, he was given his inheritance and promptly cut off.

"I'm surprised you guys all still hang out in the club."

Adam laughed, "We grew up there, no one would dare question us. Our family names are on their paychecks. That's all they need to know."

It was hard to get a word in, but when I did it was all in line with my online bio—everything he already knew. He seemed happy to be confirming his research, but he was happier telling me about his childhood, which sounded dreadful and depressing.

In my real life, I grew up without a TV. My mother felt television skewed a child's perception of reality. Real life was nothing like TV shows, and they could leave behind a messed-up concept of reality. That was covered in her first book—how damaging TV was on a child's self-concept and confidence. Scripted conversations were far from reality, and it could be challenging to discern fantasy from fact. Adam and his sister watched a lot of TV and movies. It seemed like the only thing they did together aside from the game.

Explained a lot.

We had vastly different upbringings. While my family traveled together, theirs traveled apart. My family played board games and did puzzles together. They watched sitcoms and movies. My mom was a busy working mom who was home as much as possible. His mother was a stay-at-home mom who stayed out as much as possible.

I asked appropriate questions here and there, although he didn't need encouragement to keep talking. I was entertained by his storytelling. He told them with such flourish—those funny stories every family had about the champagne bottle breaking the chandelier all over Thanksgiving dinner, or the dog stealing the ham off the dining-room table on Christmas Eve. I was fairly certain some stories were scenes from sitcoms, but I let it slide. I wondered if he thought they happened to him. My mom would have a field day with this.

We took off our shoes and walked in the stream a little. The water was cold and felt sharp around my ankles. Adam's arms were firm and muscular around my waist as he bent down and kissed me. Breathless, I felt heavy and warm. His body was solid, and I could feel the cut of his muscles through his shirt. I needed to be careful not to let things get too physical too fast.

We spent the afternoon in each other's arms. Adam was a skilled kisser, and I found myself feeling like I could just sit and kiss him forever. No harm in a little fun, it was all about control, something I was exceptionally good at.

The sun was starting to set. Not at all sure of where we were or how dark it was going to get, I looked around. I was about to say something when a woman quietly appeared, carrying thick white candles. She put them down, lit them, and returned to wherever she was hiding. I relaxed, knowing we were not about to be lurched into complete darkness. I leaned back on Adam's chest to watch the sunset. The clear skies made way for a bright and colorful evening. As the sky darkened, I tried to make a mental note of everything that happened. I could hardly wait to get home to my journal.

"This was a remarkable day. Thank you."

"You make it sound like it's over. I think not."

"I have plans in the morning with Lizzy. I'm afraid I'll need to get some sleep. Someone kept me up all night last night."

"Fair enough." He stood and took my hand, giving it a kiss before helping me up. We walked hand in hand past trees to a waiting car and van.

When we were spotted, the driver and Ruby jumped out to greet us from one car, and two ladies jumped out of the van with flashlights, scurrying past us to clean up the picnic.

The ride home was quiet, mostly because I pretended to sleep the entire way. Ruby curled up on Adam's lap and I rested my head on his shoulder. I was exhausted in every sense of the word. It was a long day, and I still had a lot of writing to do when I got home.

There was a prolonged kiss goodbye at the door but no invite in.

Sorry, not sorry, Adam. You have taken way too much of my time in the last forty-eight hours. I need a minute to collect my thoughts and catch my breath.

From the window, I watched as Adam debated leaving.

Take the hint. Get in the car and go home.

After pacing and staring at the door, he got in the car and drove away.

I grabbed a bottle of water and my journal. I needed to write as much as possible while it was fresh in my mind. With Ruby curled up at my feet, I took pen to paper. I wrote for three hours before finally going to bed. Lizzy was expected early. I needed some sleep. After a long hot shower, the full-sized bed was inviting. Ruby was a bit of a bed hog; she made me miss my king as she stretched her little body out across the pillows.

The next morning, Lizzy canceled. She said she wasn't feeling well, but I could hear Brandon in the background.

"Oh no, do you want me to come by with some soup? We can watch a movie." *Don't laugh. Don't laugh.*

"Oh, that's so sweet of you! But I'm probably contagious and just need to sleep. Don't come by!"

"OK, if you're sure?"

"Yes! I'm sure. I'll call you later. Thanks, Katie."

I could hear them laughing as she hung up. That was fine with me. I needed a little more time with my journal.

Chapter 16

"Couldn't close, huh?" Brandon couldn't stop laughing. "Even with the whole fantasy date?"

"She had plans with Lizzy this morning."

"Um, yeah, Lizzy said they had something planned." Brandon didn't volunteer any information about that.

Adam sliced the ball. "I hate golf. Why do we play?"

"You don't hate golf. You're just distracted. You hate losing." Brandon made a great shot onto the green. "Lucky for me, your sister doesn't have the same problem closing."

He couldn't resist taking that dig, and he was lucky Adam didn't take a swing at him with his sand wedge.

Adam punched Brandon's arm.

"Come on, don't hate the player; hate the game. Isn't that what you always say?" Brandon rubbed his arm.

"As long as the game isn't my sister!" Adam smiled. He knew it was not a game. Truth be told, he had seen it coming for years. The jealous way they acted with each boyfriend Brandon met and each girlfriend Lizzy was introduced to.

"Fuck this, Adam. Can we just go inside and drink? It's hot out here, anyway."

"Yeah, sure, but you're buying."

Brandon laughed. "As if anyone would charge us anything here."

As a child, everyone was enamored by Brandon's long lashes and curly blond hair. His parents always kept him within reach to use as a prop with the help of the nanny of the moment. Unlike Adam, he went through many nannies. His father took a liking to all of them, later needing to pay them off. Some with eighteen years of payments. His mom didn't care and was thrilled not to have to meet that need. His mom was also from old money, they married to connect the two families and little else. After the obligatory boy was born, thankfully on the first try, they quickly assumed separate private lives.

The club had borne witness to all of Brandon's firsts. First words, steps, kiss, and with his final nanny, an exchange student, he became a man. His father was proud when he learned of their encounter. Brandon often wondered if his dad had planned it, hiring someone too young for even him. Once free of supervision, Brandon would hitchhike, then later borrowed cars from the valet to get to the beach a mile down the road. Adam and Lizzy were his sidekicks, they had talked him into and out of many situations over the years.

Without any words needing to be spoken, the bartender served them both a highball of whiskey.

With an apprehensive sigh, Adam said, "I think I love her, man."

Brandon laughed. "The only thing you love are your clubs." Finishing up his drink, he banged the glass down on the table. "Time for the Dream Three! Let's go get you your girl."

Lizzy was waiting for them when they got home. Brandon set his laptop down on the kitchen counter next to Lizzy's. Adam placed his across from them.

"The Dream Three back again. It's been a while since we played together." Lizzy was excited to roll up her sleeves and get things moving faster with Katie.

"This isn't a game," Adam corrected her. "And I always hated that corny group name."

"Hey, I came up with that name, but you're right. This is not a game. This is for keeps. We need to focus. How far did you get with your research, Adam?" Lizzy asked.

Adam filled them in on his efforts so far. "I have the basics but didn't find anything on social media."

"She's not on social media. Something about it being mundane. I don't know. I agreed with her at the time, but now that I'm trying to find information, social media would help," Lizzy added.

Brandon, the techy one of the group, was up for the challenge. "Who's got a picture? I want to run facial recognition. Just because she doesn't have an account doesn't mean she hasn't appeared in anyone else's."

***

I was writing in my journal when the first alert rang out on my laptop in the other room, then another, and another. Technical fireworks were going off in there. I walked over and put in the passwords to view my tracking screens. It seemed like a massive effort to find out more about Katherine was underway. I poured myself a cup of coffee and got comfortable. It looked like my identity was going to be tested. Watching, I saw all the big companies' search software being used, sparing no expense. That was OK. I always planned for the big company background searches, although it was usually the free and $1.99 searches that tested my identities.

Oh, facial recognition? Fun! Let's see if I hold up to not one but several search agencies.

Facial recognition software was a lot easier to manipulate than one would think. Pretty simple but time intensive. I always took the time. I uploaded a nice, clear front face photo, then ran the recognition search on it. When the system found a match, I clicked "no" for anything that was a past identity or really me. I clicked "yes" if it was a person in the background of the picture or someone out of focus. It was OK to have a wild card here and there. Naturally, there would be obvious bad matches in the group. I repeated this process with a few search programs until a search didn't bring me up at all. The search algorithm learned that I was not a match for me and would not suggest it anymore.

Watching the different alerts get tripped pushed my background development to its limits. I was intrigued and a little curious about what sparked such a deep dive. I started making some notes. I was familiar with most of the software and services they used. I jotted down the few I didn't recognize. Did someone hire an agency? They could probably teach the government a thing or two. They left no stone unturned! I hoped Katherine Lindstorm would hold up to this scrutiny.

I needed to know what they were learning about Katherine. I would need to study the search results. I did not want to be caught off guard. For example, interestingly, a search decided Katherine grew up in the Midwest. I had to laugh. The software was working hard to put the pieces together. No red flags. Hours later, when the thorough search appeared to be exhausted, I closed my laptop and patted myself on the back. My background build held up nicely. I made note of any events or locations which were reported and waited to see who brought up something that would tip me off that they did the search.

The next day Lizzy, Chris, and I went antique shopping. At lunch, Chris casually mentioned one of the more random places in which the facial recognition search tagged me.

"I was thinking maybe we should take a trip to Gills Rock."

"Gills Rock? Never heard of it. How about you, Katie?"

"Gills Rock?" *Yup, I know where Gills Rock is.* I looked up from my menu. "I never heard of it. Where is it?"

"Oh, it's a little fishing village on Lake Michigan," Chris said, looking to Lizzy for assistance.

"Fishing? Do you fish, Chris?" Lizzy asked.

Poor Chris looked confused, and Lizzy was just letting her hang.

"Me? No, no, I don't fish. Just looks like a nice place to maybe shop and sightsee."

"Sure, I think it's a great idea, or maybe we can go to Ajo?" Lizzy countered.

"Ajo?" I asked.

"Yeah, you know, Ajo, Arizona," Lizzy said, staring me down.

"What's in Ajo?" It was hard to keep a straight face. There was nothing in Ajo except a random address that came up in the search—another small town. I couldn't have them connect me there either. I needed to direct them away from the idea of me in a small town, especially one in which a past identity lived nearby.

I decided to throw them a bone and casually mention, "When I lived in Chicago, we used to go to Cheboygan State Park. I think there's fishing there."

"I didn't know you lived in Chicago." Lizzy was clearly thrown.

"No? It's the only other place I lived before here. I'm surprised I've never mentioned it."

"I know Adam and Brandon are talking about taking a trip to Michigan to tour vineyards. Maybe we should tag along." Lizzy dropped the idea of fishing.

Chris was quick to answer with a strong voice, "No. No vineyards."

"I thought you liked the vineyards, Chris. You're still coming tomorrow, aren't you?" Lizzy looked concerned.

"Yeah, I'm coming. Are you going, Katherine?" Chris asked.

"Umm, I guess so. Adam said something about a road trip tomorrow." I was confused.

"Crap, we ruined the surprise. He arranges private tasting tours at vineyards for us every year. See what you made me do, Chris."

"No worries, I don't think it's a surprise." I attempted to save Chris.

Chris did not seem to know what to say and looked to Lizzy for direction.

I changed the subject. "Lizzy, how are the surfing lessons going?"

That was all it took. Lizzy rattled on about her favorite topic: Lizzy.

Chapter 17

Adam, Lizzy, Brandon, Chris, Matt, and I planned to meet Saturday morning at the park deli. While we waited for Matt, I watched an older man walking around talking to people, carrying flyers. He was not dressed like a politician or a salesman. I watched out of the corner of my eye as he approached person after person. This group was so self-involved they didn't notice him until he was practically on top of us trying to get someone's attention.

The flyer had a large headshot of a pretty girl. I knew that face; we all knew that face. The girl in the photo had different hair and more natural makeup, but it was clearly Tiff. The flyer even had "TIFFANY KANNON—MISSING" printed on it in large letters. They all shook their heads dismissively and continued to ignore the man. I got up to get a coffee refill and asked if anyone else would like some. I really didn't need more coffee. I followed the man with the flyers into the deli. It was my chance to get more information.

"Is this your daughter? Has she been missing long?"

"No, I'm a private investigator with G.B. Investigative Services Agency. The family hired me. Tiffany has not been back to her apartment in a couple of weeks. They had assumed she was traveling, but no one has heard from her. The only clue is a plane ticket that was purchased, but the airline has no record of her boarding the plane."

The clerk interrupted and said she looked familiar.

I wanted to hang around and hear what the clerk had to say, but I couldn't let the group spot me. When I returned to the table, everyone was standing. While I was getting coffee, Matt called and said he was not up for the trip. Time to go.

I couldn't stop thinking about Tiffany Kannon. That photo was clearly the Tiff who Adam met at the park the day I picked this project. Did they not look at the flyer? Was I missing something? We left the park, and I noticed Chris glancing back at the man with the flyers.

OK, Chris, seems like you have something you would like to say. I needed to figure out how to approach her alone about Tiff.

We loaded into a small party bus. I could see Chris was likely starting to feel like a fifth wheel. It was a long bench seat that extended the length of the bus on both sides. We could probably fit ten comfortably, fifteen legally, and twenty if we squished.

Brandon and Lizzy were all over each other at the far end. Chris was sitting opposite Adam, who motioned for me to have a seat next to him. I plopped myself next to Chris and put my legs across the aisle on top of Adam. The physical contact would make him feel valued and sitting next to Chris helped her feel less excluded. None of this got past Adam and Lizzy, who quickly turned their attention to Chris.

It was interesting how swiftly they picked up on that cue. Brandon quickly followed suit, and we were now all comfortable talking as a group. It was a three-hour drive, and Adam had several bottles of wine chilling and ready. He had chosen an assortment of older wines from the vineyard we were visiting. He said he liked to prepare himself to notice this year's changes. Before we knew it, there was music pumping, and everyone was dancing and joking. Tiff didn't even seem like a passing thought. Adam, by the way, couldn't move. He walked with rhythm, but he danced like a fish out of water, flailing around.

About two hours into the drive, the bus turned off the main highway, and the driver turned off the music. Lizzy announced a surprise stop. They all rolled their eyes and groaned. This seemed like an expected Lizzy thing. The now quiet party bus suddenly slowed down and pulled over. An excited Lizzy jumped up and ran to the door, holding my hand and dragging me.

"Just wait 'till you see! I saw it online when I was searching for things going on in the area today."

The bus door opened to reveal an estate sale. Tables were covered with once-beloved knickknacks, and blankets were covered with clothing from all ages and eras. There was no need to fake enthusiasm. It looked like a fascinating collection of random stuff. The others followed off the bus with much less interest.

Adam slid next to me, put his arm around me, and said, "Anything you want!"

I had to laugh. "Oh, Adam, you big spender! Anything?"

Not knowing if I was joking or mocking him, he went with it. "Anything for you, my dear," he said, holding his head up high and extending his arms wide. "Anything! Big or small, pretty or ugly—the choice is yours."

I held out my hand. "Twenty dollars, please." Leaving the others hanging around the bus, Lizzy and I walked around.

While Lizzy was trying to decide whether or not a pocketbook was vintage, I spotted a little girl walking around alone. She was watching people browse and keeping an eye on a small table. On the table were things that looked like they came from a child's bedroom. It was easy to see that an ugly doll was loved. It was dirty from playing and being carried around as opposed to the pretty, clean dolls and toys in excellent condition next to her.

Picking up a bracelet and the doll, I handed the woman the twenty-dollar bill and waited as she wrote out a receipt.

I thanked the lady and walked to the side of the house. I squatted under a large tree and peeked behind it. "Hi there."

The little girl was crying behind the tree. I handed her the doll. Her red, wet eyes grew big.

"Maggie!" She hugged the doll and then me. "But the lady said everything in the house had to go. It didn't belong to us anymore."

I handed her the receipt. "Well, Maggie belongs to you now."

Rejoining the group, I saw Lizzy had accumulated several bags and was in her glory. The others had barely moved from the bus, stretching their legs.

"Hey, little woman, what did you spend my hard-earned cash on?" Adam came over and put his arm around me.

I held up the bracelet. "I found this little trinket—perfect for refurbishing."

Lizzy started rattling off her many finds as we all boarded the bus. She could not wait to show me everything she got. Adam and Brandon talked about a sporting event of some kind, leaving Chris once again the odd man out.

I attempted to draw her back into the conversation. "What do you think, Chris? Didn't find anything you like?"

"No, I think sorting through other people's belongings, assessing value, and haggling over their worth is horrible."

Well, look at that—Chris had an opinion, and a strong one at that. You go, girl!

Lizzy completely missed the point of the comment. "I have to say, Katie, you overpaid for that bracelet. I can teach you a thing or two about haggling, especially at things like this. They are desperate and will take just about anything."

Brandon moved to the front and hit a few buttons, desperate to get the party started again. The music blasted, and he did a horrible impersonation of a dying donkey. He may have been trying to dance. Whatever he was doing, the mood instantly changed back, and even Chris was laughing, holding her side. It seemed like this party bus was back on track.

Finally, we arrived at our destination, a vineyard. An overly excited welcoming staff greeted us. Adam was met with handshakes and pats on the back as he introduced me like I was a prize he won at the state fair. I received welcoming hugs and kisses. The others stepped off the bus and were greeted with much colder waves and smiles.

An older man and woman came hurrying out from behind a stone wall. "Adam, you just wait! Just wait!" The older man gave Adam a firm handshake and pat on the back.

"Katherine, this is the owner and operator of Valard Orchards, Joe, and his wife, Marie."

The woman gave him a hug and nodded at me. "Come, come, I had them set up a table for you and your friends on the patio." She directed the group through stone arches around to the back of the house.

The wife shot her husband a look, and he gave her a little reassuring smile. Not sure she was a big fan of Adam.

"Adam, Joe thinks you'll love this vintage. Hopefully, you can help introduce it in the city," Marie said, showing us to the table. "Sit, relax. I have snacks to accompany the wine tastings."

A beautiful, reclaimed wood table surrounded by large, inviting chairs welcomed us.

A young girl came out and placed a cheese platter and a basket of steaming bread on the table.

"This is amazing. The view is breathtaking." I was in love with this place. There were rows and rows of grapevines and gray stone walls. The air had a sweet, fragrant smell.

"Hopefully, you feel the same about the wine," Joe said.

He began to tell us all about the vintage and started to pour sips into heavy glasses. I loved the weight of everything here. Nothing was light or frivolous;

everything was solid and permanent. And the wine? Amazing.

Adam excused himself and went into an office with the owner. Lizzy and Brandon disappeared sheepishly. I could only guess what those two were up to. Standing with Chris on a stone patio overlooking the vineyards, I was about to broach the subject of Tiff when Marie came over and offered us another glass.

She looked stressed, constantly glancing toward the office. "That Adam is a Godsend. We almost lost the vineyard. The bank wanted to foreclose when he first showed up. Said he was touring the vineyards looking for hidden gems." She smiled, holding her glass up in salute. "He saved us."

I needed more. "I knew he liked wine, but he buys that many cases?"

"He buys *all* the cases."

The woman was serious; this was no joking matter.

"Adam comes every year and buys every single bottle. The only exception is the case or two his friends pick up."

"He buys everything?"

Out of the corner of my eye I saw Chris downing her wine and nodding.

"Yes, the entire vintage. The first year, Adam bought everything from that year and a few cases containing an assortment of every vintage going back. That sale alone paid off our debts and funded the next year."

"Wow, that's amazing!" I was impressed.

"Yes, we hope his distribution will someday put our brand on the map. He's a great man." Marie blushed and waved her hands in front of her face.

Chris almost spit out her wine. "Oh yeah, he's a prince, that Adam."

Her tone went unnoticed by Marie. "I'm so sorry, I have a tendency to ramble when I'm nervous."

Without giving us a chance to reassure her, Marie scurried away, leaving Chris and I alone again.

"I had no idea Adam was a distributer."

"He's not."

"Oh, Marie made it sound like Adam distributed the wine for them."

Chris looked relieved to be interrupted by the group returning. I made a mental note to revisit the conversation later when we were alone.

Marie came back out with an order pad and we all purchased assorted cases. Joe looked pleased as he emerged with Adam, patting him on the back. He gave his wife a wink. She breathed a sigh of relief and smiled back. Such a lovely couple. I wished I could spend more time getting to know them and the family. They would make a good project someday.

The ride home was tranquil and uneventful. I pretended to sleep, hoping the group would have a conversation I could listen in on. Unfortunately, Lizzy and Brandon also slept while Chris and Adam silently played with their phones. We arrived home early and went our separate ways. Everyone seemed anxious to get someplace else, even Adam.

Chapter 18

Sunday morning, Ruby and I went for our weekly art class with Chris. Aside from the initial greetings, we didn't interact at all during class. It felt like she was avoiding me. Even Ruby wasn't getting any attention. I watched her as she smiled and talked to parents and kids about having an art show.

She was putting on an excellent performance. But the in-betweens were giving her away. Her interactions were similar to customer service representatives or telemarketers. They had a pleasant performance tone to their phone voice, but once the call ended, their voice returned to normal. Salespeople, doctors, and many professionals have the same tendencies. I could see it on Chris's face, in her eyes, and posture. She had a fake glow when addressing the kids and parents. But in between, she looked distant and withdrawn.

After class, we took our usual walk. Chris seemed distracted and quiet. I was going to try to ease the conversation toward the private investigator and Tiff—maybe mention the girl on the flyer and ask what Chris thought to see her reaction. Instead, I followed her lead. I waited to see if she would fill the silence. Someone insecure like Chris didn't like long, silent pauses, it made them uncomfortable. The fact that she made no attempt to speak made me hesitant to bring up Tiff. Chris's mind was preoccupied.

Our time together felt robotic, like Chris was on autopilot. We said our goodbyes as usual at the entrance to the parking lot. In parting, I asked, "You OK, Chris?"

Defensively, she jumped. "Yes, why do you ask?"

"No reason. I know I'm tired from all that wine."

Chris liked that answer and relaxed. She was skittish today. She walked to her car while Ruby and I walked up the path around to the overpass.

I was glad I listened to my intuition. I watched from the overpass as Adam approached Chris in the parking lot once she was alone. This was a very unexpected duo. It was too much of a coincidence that they were meeting after yesterday's run-in with the private investigator.

I couldn't hear anything the two were saying, but from my perspective, Chris's body language spoke volumes. Chris crossed her arms over her chest and backed away from Adam. She was more than uncomfortable. She appeared threatened.

She looked around feverishly, and Adam looked annoyed and impatient. Adam shook his head. He looked Chris up and down and walked away, leaving her alone in the parking lot. I watched as she melted into the car and just sat there.

I called her and watched her look at her phone and put it down. She didn't answer. She started the car and drove off.

Returning home, I paced back and forth, talking to Ruby. "Everyone at the park saw what happened with Adam and Tiffany that day. I'm positive. Even with different hair and makeup, she is clearly the same person. I can't be the only one who sees that."

Ruby barked in agreement.

"Tell me this, Ruby: Why did Adam meet Chris at the park? The two of them barely speak. Chris is just Lizzy's sidekick."

I decided to call Tiffany's family to see if I could get any information. There was only one Kannon family listed in the area, so it seemed straightforward.

A few rings later, a woman's voice said, "Hello?"

"Good morning, this is Nancy from the G.B. Investigative Services Agency. I was calling regarding your missing daughter, Tiffan—"

The woman cut me off. "You listen to me, you lowlife little piece of shit. I don't know what the hell you are trying to pull, but if you call again, I'll call the cops and have you arrested. My daughter is standing right next to me. Nice try."

I stared at the disconnected phone in my hand in shock. I was thoroughly confused. The name on the flyer was Tiffany Kannon. I was sure of it. Yes, the private investigator *said* Tiffany Kannon. I knew that at least Chris recognized her in the picture.

I decided to do a quick search on Tiffany Kannon. Google turned up a substantial social media presence, which I expected, but this Tiffany Kannon was not Adam's Tiff or the PI's Tiffany. This Tiffany was a twelve-year-old girl from a wealthy family. She didn't even look anything like the picture on the flyer, which explained the hostile reaction from her mother. The only other Tiffany Kannon I could find was an 84-year-old grandmother in Canada, again no resemblance at all. I wish I had a picture. I should have taken a flyer. *Wait, he wasn't handing out flyers. He was showing one flyer around.*

An extensive internet search turned up nothing for G.B. Investigative Services Agency. I tried every combination of abbreviations I could think of. The business name was not registered; that was for sure. If this agency was legit, their marketing sucked.

This project was turning out to be a real page-turner!

Chapter 19

The next week, everyone was remarkably busy.
Adam was receiving the wine delivery, and Chris was
avoiding me. Lizzy and Brandon disappeared off the
face of the Earth. I dropped off Ruby at doggie day care.
I was thankful they liked her and made room each time I
called. She was a little thing, give her a blanket, and she
would just sleep all day. I shook off a feeling of
separation anxiety. *Pull it together, it is a dog. She'll be
fine.*

Ann needed to spend some time around town. Plus, I wanted to bring this case of wine home to my real house. I would hate to accidentally leave it behind.

Once home, I changed into Ann. I liked Ann. She was comfortable. I just needed to tweak the look a little. I needed her to be approachable. I put on pretty glasses, wire frames, clear glass, and natural makeup. I looked like the girl next door. I'd walk around, do a little shopping, stop at the park deli, and see if I could run into that private investigator.

I started at the park deli for breakfast. No luck there, so I moved on to Main Street. I did some shopping and picked up some odds and ends. I ate lunch at the bistro and sat outside closest to the sidewalk. Nothing. At least it was a relaxing day.

Chris knew something. I thought a surprise visit later that night might be a good idea. Stopping in the liquor store, I wandered up and down the aisles looking for something to bring to Chris's apartment. I spotted a familiar label: Pasmonvin Vineyards. This was the wine from Adam's restaurant. It was a little more than I usually spend. I hesitated for a moment, but I couldn't pass it up.

Leaving the liquor store, I spotted him across the street. The large balding man, flyer in hand, was stopping people on the road. Before he saw me, I shuffled my bags around and pretended to talk on the phone while I covertly snapped photos. I did not know who this guy was, and I wasn't sure I would find him again. At least with a photo I could try to figure out his identity. Hopeful to get at least one clean shot, I continued to discreetly hit the button on my phone as he approached me.

"Excuse me, have you seen this girl?"

Taking a good look at the flyer, I adjusted the packages in my full arms and continued to hit that button. If I captured any part of this flyer, I'd be golden. "Actually, she looks familiar. Who is she?"

"Tiffany Kannon. She's been missing for a few weeks. Her family is worried."

"Oh no! I sure hope they find her. Does she live around here?"

"Someone thinks they may have seen her in the park. That's all we have to go on. I'm checking with all the store owners. Maybe she stopped in."

"If I think of anything or see her, is there a number I can reach you at? A hotline?"

"Yes, call G.B. Investigative Services Agency." He pulled out a scrap paper and gave me a local phone number.

"I will. Good luck. I hope she's OK."

"Thank you. Me too."

Something about the way he said that told me he really wanted to find her. It was personal.

We went our separate ways. I couldn't wait to put down my bags and check if I had anything usable on my phone. But it was getting late, and I needed to grab Ruby from day care. I dropped everything in my kitchen and ran to change back into Katherine. Feeling rushed, I decided to slow down. Katherine did not do anything half fast.

Breathe. Look in the mirror. Everything in place and put together? OK, Katherine, grab that new bottle of wine and a pretty gift bag, and go get Ruby. I felt guilty for leaving her for so long.

Ruby didn't care. She smothered me with kisses, and her tail wagged so hard her whole body moved with it.

"OK, girl, we need to get home. We have work to do."

A quick glance at my phone showed I'd gotten some great shots of the PI and a decent picture of the flyer. Both would need a little photoshopping to be useful but that would have to wait. Not knowing how long Adam, Lizzy, and Brandon would be preoccupied, I needed to visit Chris tonight.

"Sorry to leave you again, baby, but I need to run out."

Ruby huffed at me and walked to her bed.

On the drive over, I put together the plan in my head. I knew Chris was home alone because her favorite reality show was on at eight, and she never missed it. She told me all about it one day on our Sunday walk. I would pretend I forgot and present her with the wine. I would suggest we watch it together, and after a few glasses of wine I'd bring up the subject. I needed to be careful. Maybe ask about Adam's past girlfriends.

I knocked on her door. All was going as planned until she opened the bag and took out the wine. She turned pale and swooned. Apparently, people really did swoon.

"Are you OK, Chris?" I grabbed the bottle from her hands just in time.

"What? Yes, thank you. I'm fine. It's fine. OK, yeah. I'm fine." Chris did not seem to know what to do with herself. It was like she had short-circuited, pacing around the kitchen like a caged tiger.

"Chris, sit down. Breathe. Please sit down." I grabbed her wrist and gently tugged her into a chair. She was scaring me, and I considered texting my mom.

"I'm sorry. I'm OK. I really am." Once sitting, she collapsed into tears. Her entire body went limp, and she shuddered with each sob. I sat quietly and held her, trying desperately to figure out what could have triggered this and what I was going to do or say next. She was clearly not OK.

"It's OK. Breathe." I rubbed her back until the sobbing slowed to a silent heave.

"Oh, I can't even imagine what you must think of me." She jumped up, trying to clean her blotchy red face. "I'm so sorry."

"Chris, sit down. Talk to me. What's wrong?" I stood and got glasses from the kitchen. "Let me pour you a glass of wine."

"No, not that wine!" Suddenly angry, she got up and grabbed the bottle.

"Um, Chris, not for nothing, but that bottle was expensive. Could you please not smash it?"

"I know! That's the problem!" She held the bottle, examining the label. "What did you pay for this? How much?" Chris was finding a little backbone, and she was asserting it at me.

"It's not about the money, Chris. It's a nice bottle of wine. I thought we could share it."

"I know it's good wine." Putting the bottle down, Chris sighed. "It's a delicious wine. Just open it. Let's drink," she said, shaking her head.

I wanted to push her to explain what had just happened. She went through every emotion right in front of my eyes, but I knew better than that. I had a feeling she was a boiling pot about to blow. If I was patient, Chris was going to spill everything I needed to know before her show was over at ten.

Chris chugged the first glass of wine, making me wish I had bought something cheaper. The second glass went down slower. She started slurring by the third glass.

Slow down there. I am not going to be able to understand you when you start talking. She finished her third glass as I finished my first. The bottle was just about empty.

Easy come, easy go.

Chris barely watched her show. She seemed very preoccupied and intent on getting drunk. She jumped up out of her seat on the commercial break. "Don't worry. I have more!" She ran to the kitchen. She returned with a bottle of wine from Tranquility Vineyards. She poured two large glasses and handed me one. Taking a sip, she kept her eyes on me. I tentatively took a sip, unsure why she was watching me so closely.

"Mm, this tastes just like—"

"Yes, Katherine, yes, it does. Because it's the same wine." She paused to take another sip. "Only I paid less than one hundred dollars for an entire case."

Drinking the glass of Chris's wine, I couldn't deny it. It tasted identical. I thought it was the same bottle. "I don't understand."

"That is how your dear boyfriend makes his money. He buys out entire vintages from these small bankrupt vineyards for practically nothing. They think he is out promoting their label when what he actually does is removes their label and puts on his own fake French label. Then he sells it to restaurants and liquor stores claiming it's from the South of France. Those poor families will never see their brand on the shelves or written in a review. It's sad."

"Why do they continue to sell their entire inventory to him?"

"It's hard for them to turn down a guaranteed sale. He makes it all or nothing. He's a smooth talker, like a used car salesman. He explains that having the wine available through one source will eventually make it more valuable."

I put her bottle down next to mine. The glass bottle was identical. I didn't know what to think. If this was true, Adam did an amazingly thorough job of removing the original label.

"Wait, where are the corks?" Surely he couldn't recork the bottles. Examining the cork, I saw the branding for Pasmonvin Vineyards covered the other branding perfectly on the top. Only if you knew exactly what you were looking for and if you strenuously searched for it, you could almost see the original brand.

"Well, I'll be. That son of a bitch." I was in a bit of shock and started to feel a little bitter about the bottle of wine.

Chris was on a roll, and I was not about to stop her now. "Pasmonvin Vineyards. Do you know what that means in French?"

I shook my head. Even though I was fluent in French, I had no idea what *pasmonvin* meant.

"Ready for this?" She paused for dramatic effect. "Break it apart—*pas … mon … vin*!"

I couldn't hide my reaction. My mouth dropped, and my eyes grew big. "Not my wine! You have *got* to be kidding me! It's called Not My Wine Vineyards?"

Chris sat. "It is such a relief to share that. Please don't tell anyone about this."

"Who knows? Does Lizzy? Brandon? Matt?" I needed to know how deep this secret was buried.

Chris shook her head. "Me. And now you, I think."

That seemed odd. Why would Adam tell Chris and not his sister? "How did you find out?"

"That, Katherine, is a long, horrible story. Let me get more wine."

Chris paraphrased the best she could while downing the bottle of wine. "I heard him having an argument with this girl, Tiff, saying he wasn't doing anything wrong. He tells the winery he will promote the wine. And he does. He says he will make it an upscale in-demand brand, and he does. He never said it was going to be their name on the label. It's not his fault they never asked. That's their mistake. Adam said they should be thanking him. Without him, the vineyards would have closed years ago."

I poured more wine as Chris continued.

"Adam realized I'd heard the conversation. I didn't mean to. I wasn't spying or anything. I was just in the wrong place at the wrong time. Oh, Katherine, I have never been so afraid of a person before. The look he gave me was so cold and piercing."

"I can't imagine how you must have felt!"

"The very next day he broke up with Tiff, and that was the end of it. He pulled me aside and said there was no reason to mention the disagreement with anyone. That it didn't matter—the game was over anyway."

Another mention of the game made me curious. What did she know about the game? I hated to break her rhythm. She was on a roll, spilling big time, but I wouldn't get this chance again. "What game?"

"They take people in, make them feel important, loved. Usually they want something—an introduction, tickets to something. They choose their targets carefully. Oh my God, you are different. I'm fairly certain you're different. You feel different. You've been to the cabin. Yeah, you must be different. Don't worry."

"Oh, OK. What about Tiff? What did he want from her?"

"Nothing. Sometimes it is just cruel manipulation for entertainment when they're bored. Really mean. They are so mean. Everyone just moved on until the private investigator in the park. I don't understand why no one recognized her. It was clearly her. I was terrified to say anything and just followed everyone's lead. I can't help but worry about her."

That was all I was getting out of Chris. Her slurred words became incoherent, and her eyes were closing. "Don't tell. I know you won't tell, but don't tell."

I tucked her in. "Don't worry, I won't."

On the drive home I decided the money spent on the bottle of wine was worth every penny. It opened the floodgates. Who knew Chris was so anti-Adam? I felt like I had more questions than answers. Unfortunately, Chris was now a dead lead. I wasn't sure she had much more information, anyway. It was my experience that after someone bared their drunk soul, they closed up even tighter. She would wake up feeling relieved she had unburdened herself but embarrassed and a bit insecure. My mom had her work cut out for her.

Chapter 20

When I got home, I made a pot of coffee. I felt an all-nighter coming on. First things first—I pulled my journal out and tried to capture everything that happened with as much detail as possible. By the time I finished writing, the coffeepot was empty, Ruby was snoring, and the sun was rising. I leaned back and closed my eyes, careful not to disturb sleeping beauty. She would want a walk when she woke up, and I needed at least a solid three hours of sleep to function as a human being. I was so tired I couldn't even figure out my next steps.

Doggie day care must have worn her out because I got a refreshing six hours before she woke me up. We took a long walk together while I made a mental list. Was Adam threatened by Tiff's discovery? Where was she? But first, who was she? As the sleep cleared from my head, I remembered the photos. "Hurry up, Ruby. Mommy has work to do."

Armed with another pot of coffee, I opened my laptop and downloaded the photos from my phone. I got a few excellent pictures of the PI as he approached me. I could definitely run facial recognition on him. I wasn't as lucky with the flyer. Between weird angles, glares, and blur, there wasn't much I could do with them. Thankfully, I knew someone who could work with this image. I emailed the group of photos that showed any part of the flyer to my sister. She worked for the government, so I knew she had the technology available to her to piece together a photo.

My scan of the PI revealed he was not a private investigator. He was an accountant who lived in the next town over, George Bell.

George seemed like an everyday guy. He had a standard social media presence. He didn't change his appearance when he pretended to be a PI.

I called George at the number he gave me. He picked up on the first ring with a casual, rushed greeting. This appeared to be his personal cell phone.

"Hi, George?"

"Yes, who's this?"

"I'm calling about Tiffany."

"Is she OK? Where is she?"

"I'm calling to ask you the same thing." I took a risk and tried to catch him off guard. "I haven't seen her in a while and thought you might know where she is."

"Oh my God, no, I've been looking everywhere for her. I even started walking around with flyers saying I'm a P.I. No one has seen her. I checked hospitals and morgues. I'm starting to think I should call the police again."

"Again?"

"They said I can't report her missing because I don't have enough information about her. They said she probably went home or away on vacation and blew me off."

George felt like a dead end. "When did you last see her? Did you check with any of her friends?"

"No, that's the problem. I don't know a lot about Tiff. She answered my ad and leased my second bedroom. She moved into the apartment, and we got close, but I never met any of her friends or family. One day she just didn't come home. Just left all her belongings behind." There was a pause. "Tell me again how you know her?"

I hung up. I didn't want to get into it. It didn't seem like George knew any more than I did. I figured he made up a fake agency in hopes people would take his search more seriously. I made some notes on his address in case I needed to visit Tiffany's room and see what she had left behind.

Whatever Tiffany's story, it seemed like George cared about her well-being and not just renting out her room. Was it possible he was the only one who missed her?

All I could do was wait to hear from my sister. I hoped she could pull something from the pictures of the flyers.

Chapter 21

I knew Adam was going to be alone in the house on Monday night. Lizzy and Brandon went away for a long weekend and weren't expected back until Tuesday morning. It was time to move forward with Adam.

I knocked on his door and presented him with a bottle of Bruichladdich's X4. Made in Scotland, at 184 proof, it was the most alcoholic single-malt whisky ever made. It was surprisingly smooth. Thrilled to see me, he welcomed me in and pulled out a bottle of his finest whisky for me to try. It was official: I did not like whisky. After running around the house acting a fool in love, I could feel Adam's body starting to move slower. It was time to move the action to the bedroom.

It wasn't difficult to get him there, and I almost thought I had the timing wrong. He was suddenly moving surprisingly fast, not that I was opposed to sex with Adam. I was enjoying him, but that wasn't my goal. He almost had all his clothes off when he went down hard, face-first, on the bed. Moving his deadweight was no easy task. It took a little maneuvering, and I was thankful for my visits to the gym. I removed the rest of his clothing and made quick mental notes of any scars or weird markings. I took a brief moment to appreciate him.

Yeah, definitely not opposed to sex with Adam at some point.

I stripped and scattered our clothing around the room. In just my panties, I grabbed the shirt he was wearing and started a search of his bedroom.

Not much out of the ordinary. Adam had quite the collection of manly beauty products. He was too smart to have anything that could incriminate him or his sister in his bedroom. I moved my search out of the bedrooms and walked downstairs.

Looking around, I did a great job of making it look like we were having fun. I took a minute to grab our glasses and wash and dry them thoroughly. I couldn't have anyone taking a sip and finding out Adam's drink was laced with Ketamine. I poured some of Adam's whisky in the glasses and most of the rest down the drain, leaving the impression that we drank a lot. I left the bottles and glasses with what little there was remaining out on the counter. Having that loose end tied up, I resumed my search. Looking around the first floor, I decided the large open floor plan was not conducive to hiding anything. It also got too much traffic from friends, family, and staff.

I peeked into the garage. The garage would be convenient. Drive in, close the door, and empty the car. It was tremendous, holding six cars with room to spare. Aside from the vehicles, it was showroom clean and empty—nothing but a very meticulously arranged shelving unit with automotive products.

I closed the garage door and considered my options. They had to have stuff somewhere. The cabin contained average family stuff—keepsakes, photos, etc. They had all their clutter somewhere. The attic would be too far. They would have to transfer anything through the house and all the way upstairs. I didn't really know what I was looking for. I didn't think Adam did anything to Tiff. At least I hoped not. But somewhere buried in this house was evidence of his dirty little secrets.

Buried… the wine cellar.

A house like this had to have a wine cellar. I was so stupid. He had all that wine somewhere! I started checking doors in the kitchen.

Damn, there are a lot of closets and bathrooms. I spotted a door inside a pantry. *Bingo*. Little stone steps down.

Desperate for a light switch, I felt around on the cold walls when something hit me on the head—a pull chain. The pull chain powered up a single light bulb, revealing an exceedingly long, winding staircase. I checked my watch, thankful I still had a few hours before Adam woke up or Lizzy returned. I slowly walked downstairs.

I really wished I had my shoes or socks on; the ground was ice cold. After a quick look around, I didn't seem to leave any footprints. In fact, the steps were super clean. There wasn't a speck of dust anywhere. The further I moved from the single light bulb, the darker it got. At the bottom it was pitch black, but I could see the outline of a switch on the wall.

The switch activated a few old hanging lights. The lights were those beautiful industrial types they now fabricate and sell. But these were original and likely worth a fortune. They lit up rows upon rows of wine. It was a huge maze. I looked around, and nothing seemed excessive. It was an eclectic but standard wine collection.

I was about to give up when I felt air moving at my feet. Walking toward the draft, I found a door hiding in plain sight. I pushed around the door, and it produced a soft click and swung open. The light switch illuminated bright florescent lighting. The room was modern—dark hardwood floors, smooth-textured walls, large leather couches, and a beautiful oak and leather top bar.

A hidden tasting room perhaps?

More wines lined the walls. Hard liquors and glasses were behind the bar. I noticed yet another door. I started to feel like Alice in Wonderland, and I wasn't sure how far down this rabbit hole I should go. Another quick glance at my watch.

One last door. I was running out of time. I needed to be up in bed before Lizzy got home or Adam woke up.

Another switch powered up one hanging fluorescent light, revealing a storage room with crates and boxes all very carefully arranged. Again, nothing that would raise suspicion or seemed like an entire vineyard worth of wine.

Where the heck was it? Did he sell it that fast?

In the back corner, I noticed stacks of banker boxes marked with years in black sharpie. Last year's box seemed to be the usual crap—some pictures of the group, paperwork, concert tickets, receipts. I went back a year. The same kind of stuff—nothing out of the ordinary. As I replaced the cover on the box, my eye caught a reflection—plastic ziplock bags. The other box didn't have anything in bags. I carefully pulled it out to find stacks of wine bottle labels.

Pasmonvin Vineyards. Gotcha.

Crumpled up in the bottom of the box was a bright yellow Post-it with an address. I closed that box and reopened the other box. There were a few envelopes in this box with the same address. Satisfied with my search, I put everything back where it was and checked my path, making sure I left everything precisely the way I'd found it. I returned upstairs.

I went straight to Adam's bedroom. He was still out cold. A quick bathroom stop to make sure my feet were clean, and I messed up my hair a little. Looking at the time, I thought I might get a few minutes of sleep in, and I carefully climbed into bed. Just as I put my head down, I heard the front door. *Damn, that was close.* It sounded like they had a good time.

"Adam! You better clean this up before K gets here! I don't want to have to hire another cleaning lady! Adam! Do you hear me?"

"Good lord, Lizzy, the dead can hear you. We've been driving all night. Let them sleep. Looks like they had a fun night."

I could hear Brandon coaxing Lizzy to bed.

"This is the good stuff. Shit, they drank the whole bottle."

"Come on," Brandon whined. "Just bring whatever's left to bed. Oh, and there's a different bottle. Looks good. Just bring that."

I heard them come upstairs and retire to her room at the other end of the hall. Adam was still out. I closed my eyes, thankful to get a little sleep.

A few hours later, Adam was still out. I checked his breathing. Thank goodness he was still alive. I wondered if I overestimated his tolerance. I hoped he would wake up soon. I needed to get out of there. I threw my arm over his chest in a dramatic yawn. Nothing.

OK, Adam, no more playing nice. I gently held his nose closed. That did it.

He stirred, and I gently nudged him as we cuddled. I felt him take a deep sigh and kiss my head. I sleepily rolled over. Adam tried to get up, and I pulled him back. "No, mmm, don't go."

"I have to pee. Be right back."

While he was in the bathroom, I went downstairs and started cleaning up.

"Where'd you go? I was just a minute."

"I thought I'd make breakfast. It seems we left quite the mess."

"Yo, your sister is pissed," Brandon said. "The place was a mess, and you drank all the Macallan Edition Number Three."

"Shit, we drank all of it?" Adam rubbed his head.

"There was little left. Lizzy and I took it upstairs with us. Lizzy liked the new bottle more, anyway. So, what did you guys do while we were gone?"

I slapped Adam on the ass playfully. "Wouldn't you like to know. I gotta go get Ruby at the sitter. Brunch when Her Highness wakes?"

Brandon and Adam both nodded at me.

I ran upstairs, dressed, and collected myself quickly. I wasn't fast enough. Adam grabbed me and tried to get me back to bed. I wrapped my arms around his neck. "Mm, wish I could, babe. But I gotta go get Ruby before I lose my sitter. I'm already late." Ruby was turning into the perfect excuse.

I could see he was still feeling sleepy. I pushed him into bed. "I think we could both use a little sleep. It was a long night."

"Yeah, I am tired." His eyes were already closing. "I'll call you when we're ready for brunch."

A kiss on his forehead, and he was already out cold again.

Downstairs, Brandon had already returned to Lizzy in bed. This was going to be a slow-moving group today. Laughing to myself, I headed to the address on the Post-it note.

Chapter 22

The address was in an old industrial area. Everything was run down and boarded up. It didn't even look like the train tracks were in use anymore. Just before I reached my destination, I circled around. It looked abandoned like everything else. Unlike the buildings around it, this one had no broken windows and no trash blowing around outside. In fact, a small dumpster looked like it was in use. I debated aborting and returning under the shield of night. I was just going to have to take the chance of getting caught. I knew Adam was still home, so there was no chance of running into him. I grabbed a black baseball cap and baggy green army jacket from the trunk. Tucking my hair into the cap, anyone who saw me at a distance would assume I was a boy. I left my car a block away and walked up to the side of the building.

First, I quickly glanced into the dumpster. Inside were bags of what seems to be shredded paper. Something was going on in there. I climbed up onto the dumpster and grabbed the fire escape ladder to pull myself up. The second floor had a small window that had been left open. If I could manage my way to it, I had a way in, or at least a peek inside.

Standing on the edge of the railing, I reached the window. I pushed it open and managed to pull myself inside. Looking back, I wasn't sure I would be able to get out this way and started second-guessing my plan. I was sure there was another way out. Shit, I hoped there was another way out.

The window I came in through provided the only light. It was a bathroom—a clean, up-to-date bathroom. I cracked the door and saw nothing but darkness. There were no red security lights and no cameras or alarms. The place appeared empty. Using the light on my phone, I saw the door opened to a steel platform overlooking a massive open floor. I slowly descended the steel steps and found nothing but open space. There was even an echo. The floor was concrete. I could see a thin, light outline of garage doors. If those doors opened, there would be no place to hide. I walked deeper into the dark space and reached a wall covered by a tarp. I needed to be careful. I didn't want the tarp to fall. I wouldn't be able to get it back up, and he would know someone had been there.

The tarp was hanging from the ceiling and appeared to be attached securely. I stepped behind it to find wine crates, all with the Pasmonvin Vineyards label. Behind them were long folding tables with hanging overhead fluorescent lights. Past the tables were more crates; stacks and stacks of them in rows. Each row seemed to contain a single vineyard, organized by year. I was in awe. Chris was right, each row contained inventory spanning years from single vineyards. If you wanted wine from any of these vineyards, you had nowhere else to turn.

I saw another thin outline of a door behind the final row of crates. A quick look around the edges revealed no alarms or wires. I needed a way out, and even if it sounded an alarm, this was it. I tentatively pushed the door. Silence. It brought me to an empty, clean alley. Pushing the door closed behind me, I was careful not to leave any marks or evidence. I made my way back to my car and went home.

I needed to make notes in my journal and get at least a little sleep before brunch.

Brunch turned into more of an early dinner consisting of Chinese takeout and an old movie. Adam had a tight hold on me the entire time, and I started to feel claustrophobic in his arms. I told him I couldn't leave Ruby home alone much longer and had to go.

"I don't know why you just didn't bring her with you," he sulked.

Because I would not have the excuse to leave, you silly boy. "I didn't think of it. Next time."

"Brandon and I have a little business trip we need to take tomorrow. Call you later?"

Chapter 23

My sister called me, laughing, "Well, she's not Tiffany Kannon, that's for sure."

"I know that, dummy. Who is she?"

"No one."

"What do you mean, no one?"

"She's no one special. I mean, she is just a small-town girl. She graduated with her MBA a year ago, and it looks like she was going to take over her family business. Pretty boring stuff."

"Except that her picture is on a flyer with the name Tiffany Kannon."

"You got me there, sis. I'll send you over everything I found. It looks like you got yourself a doozy of a project. Cannot wait to hear all about it. Thanksgiving?"

"Absolutely. Thanks again. Tell Mom and Dad I said hey."

My sister really came through for me. I didn't usually ask for her help. It put her in an awkward position at work, but I was so glad I did! Tiff was not Tiffany Kannon. She was Suzie Banter. Suzie lived in Manhattan while earning her MBA at NYU. She graduated top of her class and moved home last year to take over her family business.

It was time to pay Suzie Banter a visit. Dressed like Ann, I took a drive in a dark navy rental sedan—one of those generic-looking rental cars that could really be anything. Color? Was it black? Was it blue? It depended on the light. I wish I could have brought Ruby with me for the ride, but she was memorable. I wondered if dyeing a dog's hair was a thing. Maybe a shave? How did one disguise a dog?

About a mile away, I pulled over and arranged a nail on the ground. It took only two tries to get it in the tire. Just before where the GPS said the house was, I pulled over. I made as much noise as I could, pulling out the spare and the jack. This was the middle of nowhere, and I could hear a pin drop. I really hoped someone was home.

A robust man with a full red beard appeared. "Hello?"

"Hi! Oh, my goodness! There is life on this road!"

"Yeah, it's really quiet out here. What happened? Need some help?"

Throwing my hand in the air, playing helpless, I said, "I think I have a flat."

Nodding toward the back of the car, he asked, "Spare in the trunk? I'll take care of it for you. Why don't you go in and tell the missus. She'll make you some coffee."

"No, I shouldn't bother you. I have no cell service. Can I borrow your phone to call Triple A?"

"Triple what? Nah, I got it. Really, go on in. She loves company."

"If you insist. Thank you so much."

Hidden down a narrow stone driveway was an old, white wooden farmhouse with a porch that wrapped around the entire house. I knocked softly on the porch door and was met by an older, strong, vibrant woman with kind eyes. A quick recap of the story of my flat, and she was at the stove making a pot of coffee. I sat down at the oversized kitchen table.

It was a large country kitchen. It felt like I stepped back in time. Many of the small appliances and fixtures looked old, but they were in excellent condition.

"Tell me, what are you doing out here? Did you get lost?"

With a laugh and a shake of my head, I said, "Maybe. I was following my GPS and lost the signal. I may have missed a turn. I'm heading to the Double R Farm Bed and Breakfast."

"Oh, I think I know where that is. Is that the working dairy farm in Kipling Valley?"

"Yes, that's the one! Am I far off?"

"Yup, you sure are. I remember hearing about them taking in overnight guests. A lot of work, but brilliant. I considered it. Saved their farm at the time," she said, laughing.

"Who are you talking to?" A young woman stopped in the doorway.

"Hey, Suzie, this is Ann. Pops is fixing her flat out front. Grab the pie from the pantry and come visit with us."

Yes, Suzie, come visit with us.

I was relieved to find Suzie, aka Tiffany, alive and well. If I didn't know better, I would think they were two different people. Gone were the atrocious leggings, heels, big blond hair, and heavy makeup. Gone were the contacts; she had her mom's eyes, but harder. Suzie was a stunning natural beauty, with the slightest scattering of freckles and curly red hair.

She reluctantly joined us.

"This table is gorgeous."

"It's original—built with the house. My family has lived here for generations."

Suzie rolled her eyes. "And it looks it, Mom. I've been trying to get them to remodel."

"That takes a lot of money. Besides, I like it."

"Because you don't know any better, and I'm here now."

"Big shot graduates top of her class with a master's in business and thinks she can waltz back here and change everything."

"First of all, Grandma would be proud and expect no less. Second—"

"I'm gonna stop you right there, young lady. Running and changing the business is all you, but no one said you could change the house."

I loved the banter. I could see the love and admiration they had for each other. I didn't get it. *What were you doing playing dress up with Adam?*

I laughed with them. "Oh, that's so exciting. Congratulations! Are you going to retire now?"

"Eventually. I get to stay *in the house*." She smiled at Suzie.

"No one said you had to leave. Don't be so sensitive."

"We have a tradition: The new generation takes over when ready or needed. I have to step back and let her do what she wants, even if I don't agree."

"Grandma let you. No questions asked. Sink or swim. My turn."

Suzie walked over and wrapped her arms around her mom. "I know how hard you worked. You just cannot question everything I say and do. Give me a little growing room. You know I still need you here and at the vineyard. Just let me buy a damn dishwasher, OK?"

"OK, fine, but no more of all this family drama in front of our guest."

I laughed. "Are you kidding? I feel right at home. I love it. Did you say vineyard?"

"Yes, our family has the distinct honor of being the first female-owned and operated vineyard in the U.S. Each generation takes over, no questions asked, in honor of my great-grandmother, who took the business over and turned it around from her alcoholic father."

Oh shit, that sounds familiar.

"Tranquility Vineyards. Maybe you've heard of us?"

"I'm sure she hasn't, Mom. Let's not get into that now."

"Sorry, we don't usually air out laundry in front of guests," she said with an awkward laugh.

"It's OK, Mom. My mom has been selling to this guy."

"A distributor. He's a distributor."

"Who has been relabeling the wine as his own. She doesn't believe me."

"I don't think you appreciate all that he's done for us."

"Yeah, right. If he's so wonderful, why won't he let us out of the contract?"

I wanted to keep them talking and asked, "Contract? I'm no lawyer, but don't they all have loopholes?"

Suzie looked determined. "Sure, they do, all for his benefit. My friend from graduate school *is* a lawyer. She said she'll work on it for me. She just needs evidence."

"Which you couldn't get, Suzie." Her mom wanted to drop the subject.

"No, I got a full-out confession, not that anyone will ever believe me."

"All fixed!" Pops entered the kitchen and stepped up to the sink to wash his hands.

Bad timing, but I had gotten all I needed from this family. I said my goodbyes and got the unneeded directions to the bed and breakfast.

Thankfully, when my sister called, I was alone in the car driving home, trying to work out the project's next steps.

"Big Mac called me and wanted to know what you were working on."

"What did you tell him?"

"I told him you were on sabbatical. He said bullshit. Apparently, your project is his case. You better give him a call."

She hung up. She probably thought this call would upset me, but I couldn't have been happier. Big Mac, as I called him because of his obsession with McDonald's, was a thin little guy with the FBI, named Steven. We had worked a case together years ago and became great friends, but he didn't know about my side projects.

When I got back to the house, I sat and read through my journal, wondering if I had enough to end the project and explain this to Big Mac without letting him in on my secret. I wanted to talk to him and see what he knew.

I texted him: "Golden Arches, 5 a.m."

He responded with a thumbs-up emoji.

Chapter 24

The next morning at four thirty, McDonald's bag in hand, I walked over to our bench. Unsurprisingly, he was already waiting. When we worked together, this was our meeting point, right by the bridge entrance and a McDonald's. It wasn't a proper park. It was more of a rest stop—a skinny trail with a few scattered benches along the water.

I placed the bag between us and sat next to him.

Opening the bag, he laughed. "Who do you know at McD's? They wouldn't make me one."

I smiled; I missed him. Resisting the urge to give him a proper bear hug, I looked out at the bridge. I didn't make eye contact, and neither did he. Neither of us was sure what the other was working on, if we were alone, or if we were being watched.

"Whatcha got?"

Straight to the point. He was in a rush.

"You first. I got you a Big Mac."

There was that laugh again. He let out a sigh. "We can't seem to connect all the dots, but your pretty boy moves a lot around. Is he the one who knocks?" he paused and looked at me. I didn't get the reference, so he quickly moved on. "He and his country club buddy both seem to be spending a lot for unemployed people."

I knew what he was trying to say. It seemed my two friends were not particularly good at money laundering. I laughed. "I can help you with that."

"The best news I heard all day."

"First, I need something."

"Anything for you."

I touched his hand as I got up. "Always good to see you. I'll be in touch."

Making my way home, I decided the project was over. Time to clean up. I made a call. "One week out."

"Gotcha."

Chapter 25

The next day was Sunday, and I met up with Chris as usual. I was a little sad knowing this was the last time. I really enjoyed our time together. She had really grown into a more confident person. I wanted to make sure Katherine didn't leave her flat and feeling abandoned.

"I don't know, Chris. I just can't help thinking you're such an amazing artist. Why don't you do this for a living?"

She chuckled. "I guess because I don't need to."

"Exactly! You don't need to be a starving artist. You could go anywhere, live comfortably, and throw yourself into being an artist full time. I can just see you living in an art studio, happy and selling art, like in San Fran or SoHo. You could continue to volunteer teaching at a youth center…" Just like that, I saw it on her face. She liked the idea. Probably thought about it before.

"I couldn't. Lizzy would be lost without me."

"You mean the same Lizzy who just went away with Brandon?"

"She did?"

She was hurt. "She didn't tell you? She was probably just busy and forgot." I stopped walking and looked at her. "I think Lizzy would be just fine. In fact, I think if Brandon suggested moving to the North Pole, she'd jump without a second thought." I laughed. "That girl is head over heels."

I started walking again. Chris did not. I stopped and turned to her. "What's wrong?"

"Oh, you are so right. Lizzy has Brandon now."

Her face relaxed as she slowly smiled and then laughed. "I'm free."

"Chris, are you OK? Do you need to sit down?" I was honestly concerned I was witnessing another psychotic breakdown. Maybe I pushed too hard.

"Sit down? I need to pack!"

I must have been witnessing a breakdown.

Chris grabbed me and gave me a hug.

"I've been thinking about this for a while. I don't want to be here. I don't want to be in this friend group. I want more. I want my own life. I'm tired of following her around."

"Wait. What?"

"Oh, I'll miss you. But you will visit me, right?"

This was easier than I thought.

"Don't tell anyone. I'll just send them a postcard from France."

"France?"

Laughing, she picked up Ruby, giving her a kiss. "I'll miss you too."

On Monday, I arrived home from a walk with Ruby to find Adam sitting on my front porch on a new rocking chair.

"There you are!" He greeted me with a kiss and a bit of unwelcomed groping.

"The first time I saw you on this porch, I thought you needed a second rocking chair—for me."

Do not eye roll. Just smile. "That's so sweet of you! Thank you!"

"Whatcha up to?"

I smiled. *Oh, if you only knew, Adam. If you only knew.*

"Nothing; thinking of grabbing a bite. You?"

I opened the front door, and we went inside together. I opened a water bottle and poured half into the dog's bowl.

"I thought we could take a hike. I want to ask you something."

Good Lord, Adam, what do you want? "Sure, let me grab my boots."

Adam took me back to the waterfall. I didn't mind; it was relaxing there.

"No backpack?" I was disappointed. I was kind of hoping for that chicken salad one last time. I needed to get the recipe somehow.

We walked down to the falls, hand in hand, and I stopped dead in my tracks. There was a small bistro table set up with two chairs. The setup looked like it was pulled right out of a five-star fine-dining restaurant and plopped at the edge of the waterfall.

With a Cheshire grin, he pulled out a chair for me to sit. Confused, I obliged.

As he sat down, a waitress appeared out of nowhere with a bottle of wine and poured us glasses. The look on his face—he was so proud of himself.

Following the waitress was a man in a tux and white gloves, carrying a large silver tray with a single black box on it.

Adam took my hands. "Katherine Lindstorm, I know we haven't known each other long…"

What the fuck?

"But I want you to know this isn't something I often say. Never, in fact."

Oh my God, Adam, just stop.

"I love you. I'm one hundred percent head over heels in love with you. Don't panic. I'm not proposing. Not yet."

Not yet?

"I just need you to know that I see a future with you. You make me so happy."

"Adam, you don't know enough about me to love me. You don't love me. You love you when you're with me. There's a difference."

"I don't understand. How is it a bad thing that you make me a better person?"

"Don't you hear yourself? It's all about you. The way you feel—the person you are. What about me?"

Adam was frustrated, and it showed as he raised the volume of his voice.

"What about you? I don't understand! I love you." Then in a mumble, "This is not going the way I planned. Why are you doing this to me?"

"Oh, Adam, I'm not doing anything to you. Thank you. This is such a thoughtful grand gesture." Aware that not accepting his gesture was embarrassing for him, I stood and hugged him with a huge smile. A few hikers stopped and applauded, probably thinking this was a proposal, which thankfully, it was not. Their attention, along with my thanks, seemed to make him happy and utterly unaware I hadn't returned his confession of love. Fine by me.

On Tuesday, Adam and I had a double date with Lizzy and Brandon. Lizzy fawned over the bracelet Adam gave me as a symbol of his love. It was a simple brunch cut short when Brandon received a text.

Wednesday, I got a frantic call from Lizzy. She was sobbing and screaming on the phone. I could hardly understand her.

"Slow down, Lizzy. What happened?"

"They came, Katie. They came and took everything—everything!"

Yup, I know. "Lizzy, what are you talking about? Who came and took what?"

Nothing but sobs on the other end of the line and ramblings about her clothing and jewelry. "Lizzy, let me talk to Adam. Where's Adam?" I knew where Adam was: sitting next to Brandon in handcuffs. I couldn't help but smile.

"They took him too!"

Thursday morning, I had pulled out my bag and started to pack when there was a knock at the door. I hoped it was the sweet neighbor with some homemade banana bread. I was going to miss her little baking gifts. I glanced at the clock. Shit, it wasn't even seven.

At the door I was met with a hug and a cup of coffee. Adam casually walked in, closing the door behind him.

"Adam! What a surprise. What's going on?"

"I can't surprise my girl with coffee?"

He walked around the apartment as he talked, looking around.

"I made it myself. Did I use enough honey, honey?"

He didn't. It was horrible coffee. I immediately regretted the large gulp.

Walking into the bedroom, he stopped at the bag on my bed.

"Are you going somewhere?" he whispered.

I couldn't respond. I suddenly couldn't find any words, and my tongue felt big.

"Shit, OK, I may have used too much. Come sit down."

As I sat in the chair, I watched Adam as he tossed things in my bag. Ruby was barking. I couldn't move. That son of a bitch drugged me.

I felt hot. A warmth spread across my entire body, eventually breaking into a sweat. I thought I was going to be sick.

"She's waking up. Thank God!" It sounded like Lizzy.

"Here, give her a bag. She's probably gonna puke," said Brandon.

I wanted to open my eyes, but they were not cooperating. I took a deep breath. Brandon was right. I was gonna puke. I reached out, grabbing a plastic bag just in time.

"It's OK. It's OK. It's all going to be OK." Lizzy was trying to help me.

I felt an immediate release of pressure, and a fog in my head cleared as soon as I vomited.

I took a quick look around. I was in the back seat of an SUV. Adam and Brandon were up front. Lizzy sat next to me. I couldn't see where we were, and I had

no idea how long I was out. I sighed and closed my eyes.
I needed a minute.

"Brandon, she's out again. Is that normal?"
Lizzy gave me a little nudge.

"Yeah, she's fine. We'll give her a few minutes
before making her get up."

With my eyes closed, I could listen in and try to
figure out what was going on. I was not restrained or
gagged. I peeked out the corner of my eyes. The sun was
setting. Shit, I had been out all day.

"When are we stopping again, Adam?" Lizzy
whined.

"When we're running low on gas. Not a second
before." Brandon answered.

"I really don't understand why we couldn't go to
the airport." Adam complained.

"Sure, let's take your drugged girlfriend on a
flight. Think. Besides, we don't know if the airports are
looking for us." Brandon explained with a note of
authority, he was in charge.

They were running, and I was still Adam's
girlfriend. Best news I had heard all day. They didn't
know I was the one who tipped off the FBI.

I opened my eyes, holding my head in my hands.
"What the fuck?"

"There you are! You're up! She's up." Lizzy was annoyingly chipper and loud.

"Give her some water," Brandon said, passing back a bottle.

Water had never tasted or felt so good. The cold crisp of it in my mouth, down my throat—I couldn't get enough. I could feel my body temperature begin to regulate.

"What the fuck happened? What is going on? Where are we?"

"I can explain when we get there. I didn't know what else to do." Adam looked at me in the rearview mirror.

Brandon turned around in his seat. "You had us scared there for a minute. Wasn't sure if you were gonna wake up. Jackass here gave you more than half the bottle!"

"You didn't tell me how much."

"I said a drop or two, you ass."

"Well, if she takes a sip, how am I supposed to get a drop in that sip?"

Brandon shook his head. "You can be so stupid."

"You drugged me, Adam?"

"Yes, but I had a good reason. You were not supposed to be out cold an entire day. Just agreeable. I needed you to come with me quickly, no questions asked."

"An entire day? Wait, what? Why? Where are we? Shit, my head hurts." It felt like my head was in a vice. "Adam, where are we going?"

"See? So many questions. I will explain later. Please just relax. We're almost there."

Looking around outside, I couldn't imagine what he meant by *there*. I didn't recognize anything.

We were speeding along an empty highway.

"This is a decent plan, Brandon. Smart setup. I bet it was that fucking Tiff. Text them that we're about fifteen minutes out? Hey, Kate, is there anything you need?" Adam looked on edge, driving and talking fast.

"Need? For what? I still don't know what the fuck is going on."

"You haven't eaten all day. Brandon, get her a ham, cream cheese, red onion, and tomato on a toasted roll. That sound good, honey?"

Damn, it does. I was starving and acutely aware I needed bread to settle my stomach.

"Yeah, thanks."

So, they were blaming Tiffany. Being confrontational was not working, and I was not in immediate danger.

I looked in the back and spotted Ruby in a crate comfortable and happy with her tail wagging and my bag. "Who packed for me? I hope I have something more than underwear to put on."

"Don't worry. Adam started to panic a little, so I came in and packed while the guys put you in the car. Thank goodness too. He had the most random things!" Lizzy rattled off things she was smart enough to pack for me. It was way too much for my head to take.

Where was my journal? Did any of them see it? No, they couldn't have. "Where's my phone?"

"I'm sorry—we had to leave it behind." Adam looked worried.

"I still don't understand why we can't have our phones. Brandon has a phone." Lizzy complained.

"It's a burner." Adam sounded impatient; I guessed they had this conversation already.

"I don't understand what that means."

"Lizzy, I told you—they can track our phones." Brandon sighed.

"Who are they?" I had to play stupid. I knew who they were: McD and his friends. They must have been looking for them. I wondered if they had a tracker on their cars. I hoped they didn't miss this one.

"Katie, I promise it's all going to be OK." Adam was trying to keep me calm.

I wasn't going to get anything out of Adam until he was ready. Not much I could do until I got to a phone.

We turned off the highway on to the service road and then on to a dirt road. The road was throwing Lizzy and I around in the back seat. I was going to be sick again. Adam stopped the car, and Brandon jumped out and ran ahead. He moved a chain blocking a driveway, and Adam pulled in. Brandon replaced the chain and jumped back into the car. The two of them were all smiles. One would think we were off on a vacation.

The long dirt driveway ended at a large rusty airplane hangar.

What the fuck?

Everyone jumped out of the car, excited and talking all at once. The drugs made me feel sluggish, and I struggled to follow the conversations. An older man stepped out of the hanger and handed Adam a paper bag. He began unloading the car. He was stronger than he looked. I couldn't help but think he looked familiar—something in his eyes. Shaking it off, I took the bag from Adam and sat on a rock. The paper bag held a much-needed sandwich. After a couple of tentative bites, I devoured it. Reaching into the bag, I pulled out some napkins and noticed a ketchup packet. I let out a sigh of relief. It had the golden arches on it. It must have been a sign from Big Mac.

Glancing around, the place looked rundown and abandoned. Adam sat next to me with a big smile. "Ready for an adventure?"

What alternate reality are they living in?

"Adam, I think you need to start talking."

"I'm sorry. I know once we're settled, you'll forgive me."

"Settled? Settled where? Where are we going? What's going on?"

"Brandon and I are disappearing for a while and decided you and Lizzy could come along."

What? He made it sound like they were going on a business trip.

"Disappearing? Where? For how long? I have plans tomorrow."

"Plans change."

"Adam, start talking."

"OK, listen, so there was a little misunderstanding. Brandon and I were selling some inventory and didn't claim it on our taxes. I mean, if you sell one of your bracelets on eBay, do you claim that to the IRS? It is just a little bit of a mess. So, while our lawyers fix things, we're going to take a little vacay. I really am sorry I drugged you. We didn't have time to talk it over. We just needed to hit the road."

"This all seems like a lot of effort for a misunderstanding."

Seems excessive for tax evasion too.

"I would have called first, but Brandon said he didn't know if your place was bugged."

"Bugged? Why would my place be bugged?"

There was a rumbling down the road, growing louder and closer. I could feel a vibration under my feet as a large box truck pulled up. Two young guys who looked like bodybuilders jumped out and greeted Brandon. They were all business—no smiles.

"Be right back." Adam ran off and shook the newcomers' hands, patting them on their backs.

They opened the back of the truck and started unloading crates into the hanger. I walked over to the door and saw a cargo plane inside the decrepit hanger being loaded with our stuff and the crates. Lizzy bounced over to me.

"Hey! Exciting, isn't it?"

"You said Adam and Brandon were gone. I'm so confused."

She waved it off. "Adam said it was all a misunderstanding. He and Brandon got it all worked out. I overreacted."

No, Lizzy, you did not.

We stood and watched the two truck drivers load the plane. Inside, the old man walked around the plane and checked it. I assumed he was the pilot. Adam and Brandon were hanging out, laughing, and chatting. Once the plane was loaded, Adam called to us that it was time to go.

I looked around. The truck was pulling away. There was no one else anywhere in sight.

I was sweating. The pilot asked if we were ready. Adam gave a thumbs-up. Shit, I did not want to board this plane.

"Wait, I need to pee. Is there a bathroom?"

"I'm sure there's one on the plane," Lizzy chimed in.

The pilot walked by. "Nope, it's a cargo plane. No bathroom. You're lucky there's a place for you all to sit."

Brandon was getting antsy. I could see him looking at his watch.

"I'm sorry, ladies. You're just gonna have to hold it. We got to go now."

"Brandon, I'm sure we have a minute for the girls to run. Honestly, I sorta need to pee too." Adam tried to be helpful, to no avail.

"Everyone. Get on. The fucking. Plane. We have to go."

"Alrighty, I'll get the door." The pilot went over and pulled open the large hangar door with a loud rumble and squeak. The hangar was flooded with a blinding glare from the setting sun.

Shadows and movement revealed dozens of armed agents in full black combat uniforms and body armor.

Adam and Brandon both turned and started running toward the door. I grabbed Lizzy's arm and threw her to the ground with me. "Lay flat. Arms out—don't move," I whispered to her.

She looked terrified. There was shouting and running all around us. One set of combat boots stopped at us. Looking up, I saw an agent with a gun pointed at us. "Don't fucking move."

Adam and Brandon didn't get far. Adam stopped on a dime the instant someone told him to drop to the floor. Brandon, bless his heart, thought he had a chance on foot. It took all my self-control to not laugh as I watched an agent calmly taser his ass. We were all placed in handcuffs and lined up at the back wall. Lizzy was sobbing. Adam had a stone-cold blank stare, and Brandon was crying, but that could have been because the taser left a bit of a sting. The pilot sat quietly with his head down. I took it all in, making mental notes and trying to figure out what the hell was going on.

An agent unloaded one of the crates. As I expected, the crate contained wine, but under the wine the agent pulled out a brick-sized package. Using a knife, he pulled out a sample and placed it in a test tube. The substance immediately turned orange. Meth? I sure as hell was not expecting that. A fleet of black sedans pulled up, and we were all loaded into individual cars. I could see up the road where the truck was stopped, and the drivers were in custody as well. Lizzy, Brandon, and Adam's cars drove off one at a time. My sedan's door was opened, and I was uncuffed by an agent. I saw the pilot also being uncuffed. With a smile, he walked over to me.

"You age well, Big Mac."

"Aw, come on, it's a good disguise. You recognized me?"

"If it wasn't for the ketchup packet, I wouldn't have even thought to look for you."

"I wanted to make sure you didn't try to run or delay the flight. We needed to get all the crates loaded."

"Did you know they were gonna drug me?"

"No, I knew you were with them when Brandon called and ordered that ham sandwich. Cream cheese? Who puts cream cheese on a ham sandwich?"

"Mac, what the hell is going on?"

"Come on, I have some coffee in my car. Probably still hot."

We walked through teams of agents with their respective agencies on their chests. A few waves and nods from some agents who recognized me. Thankfully, the coffee was still hot.

"Do you need medical? How are you feeling?"

"Nah, I'll be fine. This coffee was definitely needed. I don't know what he gave me, but it knocked me on my ass."

Almost on cue, a medic and an agent walked over. "Real quick, we need to get blood, saliva, and a time statement from you."

"Yeah, sure. Last I remember was seven a.m.— it was in coffee. Woke up maybe fifteen or twenty minutes before our arrival."

The medic took some quick samples and handed me a urine cup.

"Wait, is there a bathroom?"

Laughing, Mac answered me. "I'd be more than happy to accompany you to a nearby bush."

"Thanks, Mac."

The medic was confused. "Um, that wouldn't be sanitary specimen conditions. I would rather you use the actual bathroom in the hangar."

Mac and I looked at each other and burst out laughing. "Shit, I really do need to pee." I returned from the bathroom and gave the medic my sample. "Come on, Mac, give it to me."

"This has been a hell of a ride. I'm sure you know. Those two have been on everyone's radar. Lots of cases leading to them, but no proof. They thought they could hide behind layers of corporations and family money. Brandon's family cut him off after he refused to work for the family business. He made some good investments initially, but they went belly-up. He watched one too many episodes of *Breaking Bad* and thought it would be a good DIY project."

"Shit Mac, you asked me if he was the one who knocks. How did I miss that? We quoted that scene from Breaking Bad a million times! Go on," I said, laughing.

"Brandon found himself a chemist who was tired of working for big pharm and made him a sweet deal to produce product. That guy was easy to find. Connecting him to Brandon, not so easy."

"I can't imagine Brandon being that smart."

"He surrounded himself with people who knew the business, old timers. Retired experts. They advised him and kept their hands clean. No one we brought in knew who he was. He found out his buddy was doing this little wine deal and roped him into expanding it and using it to help move the drugs. Seriously, it was one hell of a web. It'll take all the agencies a while to sort it all out."

I shook my head. "I can't believe I missed all this. I only knew about the wine."

"Don't be too hard on yourself. If it weren't for the evidence you gave us on the wine operation, we never would have been able to bring them in. We knew that once we got them in custody and scared them a little, they would look to protect the product. The fact that it's packaged with their wine is the best-case scenario. When they were brought in for tax evasion, they both admitted to relabeling and selling it without a distributer license. They claimed to have no employees and that they alone did all the relabeling, packing, and distributing of the wine as a hobby. They had signed contracts with all the vineyards, giving them absolute right to do anything they wanted with the wine."

"You're shitting me. Are you serious?"

"Armed with their corporate lawyers, they insisted they were doing nothing wrong. That was probably their first fatal mistake—not hiring a criminal lawyer. They laughed the entire thing off, thinking they were getting one over on everyone. The corporate lawyers had no idea we were looking for anything else."

"So, you let them think they were bailed out by their fancy lawyers and followed them?"

"Man, they were easy. Before they all tossed their cell phones, Brandon made a call to set up the plane."

I laughed hysterically. "Morons."

"That's for sure. All right, now you."

"Me?"

"Come on, sabbatical? Who are you undercover for?"

Still hazy from the drugs, I wasn't sure I could pull off a decent explanation.

"Hey, you got a call." Saved by a random agent shouting and running over, phone in hand.

"For me?"

He handed me the phone.

"Sorry, Mac, one sec. I have to take this."

I walked away for a little privacy, unsure of who would be calling me at a crime scene I should not be at.

"Hello?"

"Don't say anything. Shit, are you OK? No, don't say anything. I know you are. God damn you. You just about gave me a heart attack." It was my sister.

"I'm OK. I'm OK. Just a hell of a headache."

"This is it. No more fucking projects. I'm serious."

"Headache, remember? Please don't yell at me"

"You're so fucking lucky I covered your ass. You owe me. Oh, you owe me."

"Seriously? I love you." I could've cried. I was so relieved.

"You're undercover Homeland Security. They have nothing to do with this. I said you were checking out an anonymous tip."

"Sweet, that's perfect. You are a lifesaver, and your call literally came just in time. Love you."

"Yeah, whatever. I better be mentioned in this project, and I don't mean a vague one-line 'thanks to my sister' bit like the others." Click.

The bitch hung up on me. Shit, she could have anything she wanted for covering my ass like that.

I walked back to Mac, handing the phone to the agent.

"Well, who was that?"

"Come on, you know. My sister wanted to say how much she loves me and how glad she is that I'm OK."

"Your sister? She tore you a new one, huh?" he asked, laughing.

"Yup. How stupid must I be to get myself drugged?"

"To be fair, you did get yourself drugged. OK, story time. What are you doing here?"

"I was just following a tip for Homeland and got lucky."

"Homeland? Sure, OK, don't tell me. I only saved your life."

"How did you save my life?"

"I got you a sandwich, didn't I? I brought you coffee."

An agent walked over. "Hey, we need you. Break's over. There's a car waiting to take you to the hospital. They want to put an IV in you. Policy and all."

"Love you, Mac."

"Love you too."

They kept me overnight; I slept most of the time. Adam drugged me with twenty times the dose I had used on him. The agent who brought me to the hospital offered to take Ruby for the night and pick me up the next morning. He had kids who had been asking for a dog. They were thrilled to have the overnight guest.

By the time I got home, I was very anxious to write. I dropped everything and spent the day feverishly making notes on everything I could remember, stopping only for Ruby or me to pee.

The next morning, I found a note in my mailbox: "Park deli—11:00 a.m."

At the park deli, I spotted Lizzy immediately. She was dramatically dressed in an oversized hat and sunglasses. It was her idea of hiding.

"Katie! Thank God!" She went to give me a hug and stopped herself. Looking around, she sat down. She handed me a coffee.

Nope, not gonna drink it. Sorry, not sorry. Too soon.

"I don't understand what's going on! The FBI? DEA? ATF? The whole alphabet. I don't even know who they all are. Like, what? Seriously? They said *we* can't travel *anywhere*, not even to the cabin or a hotel. I spoke to the lawyers. They said we shouldn't talk to anyone. We just have to lay low."

"This is insane! Are you OK?"

"At least we have each other. Well, we can't see each other until this is all cleared up. The lawyer said we shouldn't talk to each other, and we can't visit or talk to the guys, no matter what! Not even a letter."

"OK, whatever they want us to do."

"I just hope this is all over in time for my trip next month. They can't expect me to cancel. Brandon and I have plans."

Poor Lizzy—completely and utterly clueless. I didn't think Lizzy knew about the drugs, even now. She seemed to think this was all an inconvenient misunderstanding. I knew for a fact she was also under investigation, spending red-flagged money. Looking around, I wondered if she was being followed. Big Mac was working on crossing all his t's and dotting all his i's before bringing her back in.

After my brief meeting with Lizzy, I took a final look around and locked up the house that served as Katherine's home. With the project coming to an end, it was time for Katherine to disappear. I told Lizzy I was going to lay low, per her suggestion. She was making it so easy for me to disappear. The timing was also great for Chris. Lizzy was so worked up she wouldn't notice Chris had left the country Sunday. I had to sign an affidavit that Chris was not involved in any way. They didn't have anything on her but the timing of her one-way ticket out of the country was suspicious.

I leisurely tossed my bags and Ruby's bed in the back of the Uber. Pulling away from the curb, I called my mom. "I'm about to go off the radar. The project was perfect. You will not believe it. You have to wait. I don't know how long I'll be gone—three to five weeks probably. No, my agent will be the only one who can reach me. Love you too. See you on the other side."

Chapter 26

Per my request, Big Mac contacted all the vineyards. A PR company was hired to help them reclaim their labels and their followings. The bottles still in Adam's or Brandon's possession were eventually returned to the original vineyards. When the drug bust was leaked to the press it was big news. Its notoriety helped relaunch all the brands and put them on the map. The wine spoke for itself, and people were thrilled to pay less for it. The vineyards were able to get more than twice what they got from Adam.

I started freelancing again as a supervisory special agent for the National Center for the Analysis of Violent Crime (NCAVC), aka criminal profiler. Only my mom, sister, and agent knew about my secret projects. Since college, I had inserted myself into situations and groups; then wrote about them under pen names. All extraordinarily successful best sellers, but none were anywhere close to this one.

Although all my novels were based on true events, this was the only one that advertised it on the cover. I don't usually use the same pen name as the identity, but it seemed appropriate in this case. With the tabloids and news picking up the trial, it was a best seller out of the gate. Everyone wanted to know more. As usual, all interview requests were denied. The identity of mysterious author Katherine L. added to the allure. Two years later, the movie was released.

Epilogue

Ruby and I sat on my balcony and watched as a storm rolled in over the water. She shook at the distant sound of thunder. I would need to make sure all the windows were secured before it beat down on the shore.

At the sound of the doorbell, Ruby ran toward the door with an annoying, welcoming bark I had grown to love.

I answered the door, and my best friend Sam stood there with a huge smile. She thrust her hand in my face.

"I couldn't wait another second!" The engagement ring was blinding.

"Sam!" We embraced forever, rocking back and forth, crying together. "Who's the lucky guy? And why am I just hearing about him?"

We moved the lovefest inside, and I opened a bottle of wine as she filled me in on all things James. He was her soul mate, and she didn't want to jinx it by telling anyone before now.

Ruby jumped up again and ran to the door seconds before the doorbell rang.

Sam jumped up. "That's him! I hope you don't mind. He's about to become your new second best friend." She answered the door while I took dinner out of the oven.

I turned around. An unmistakable pair of green eyes met my gaze. My mind started spinning.

Adam?

THANK YOU

Writing a book can be a rollercoaster of emotions. I am fortunate enough to have family and friends who support and believe in me, especially when I didn't. This book would not be possible without every one of you.

First of all, to my daughter's Samantha and Jessica: without the both of you, this book would not have gotten past the first few pages. Your excitement and interest encouraged me to continue writing. I appreciate all your thoughts and opinions.

Samantha, thank you for painstakingly reading and rereading this novel in dozens of different formats and editing stages. Sharing this process with you has been amazing.

Jessica, thank you for lending me your creative eye and grammar policing.

My husband Arnel: you believed so strongly that I would finish that you refused to read it until it was complete. Thank you for supporting me and encouraging me to finish what I started.

Mom, thank you for your support, encouragement, and buying everything I publish.

To my Aunt Marie: thank you for fostering my creativity and imagination.

Sheri, Thank you for your constant encouragement and inspiration.

Shout out to my brother-in-law Rich. You encouraged me by starting to read it and refusing to finish because you wanted to wait to enjoy the fully finished product.

Chloe, thank you for sticking me with needles and kicking my butt into gear when I strayed.

To my little test group: thank you for eagerly reading printed out chapters from a binder. Your interest in reading more, even when it was unedited and full of typos, kept me going.

To the fantastic staff of Write My Wrongs. Thank you for suffering through tense and POV issues on top of grammar and spelling atrocities. Your gentle but firm feedback and direction made this possible.

All the writers in the Long Island Writers Group: your passion for writing is inspiring.

I want to thank EVERYONE who encouraged me or offered any feedback. I heard it all, and it meant something.

Made in the USA
Middletown, DE
14 July 2021